THE BOXCAR CHILDREN®

CREATED BY
GERTRUDE CHANDLER WARNER

GREAT
4
ADVENTURE

THE SHACKLETON SABOTAGE

THE BOXCAR CHILDREN®

CREATED BY
GERTRUDE CHANDLER WARNER

GREAT
4
ADVENTURE

THE SHACKLETON SABOTAGE

STORY BY
DEE GARRETSON AND **JM LEE**

ILLUSTRATED BY
ANTHONY VanARSDALE

SCHOLASTIC INC.

ISBN 978-1-338-31704-6

12 11 10 9 8 7 6 5 4 3   19 20 21 22 23

Printed in the U.S.A.   40

First Scholastic printing, November 2018

Illustrations by Anthony VanArsdale

Contents

CHAPTER

Connecting the Dots

Henry Alden traced his fingers over the colorful patterns painted on the boomerang. He sat with his two sisters, Violet and Jessie, in the comfortable cabin of the Reddimus Society's private jet. The children had just received the boomerang in a package, and they knew it held a clue that would lead them to the next stop on their journey. But none of their clues had been as beautiful and detailed as the boomerang.

Benny, the youngest Alden, was interested in the boomerang, but he couldn't stop looking out the plane window. Below, Bangkok, Thailand, grew smaller and smaller in the distance. He watched the city as it disappeared behind a layer of puffy clouds. Then he turned in his seat to look at the boomerang too.

"There are so many dots," he said.

There really were. Black and white dots formed wavy lines. Other dots were the colors of the sunset, orange and red. The bright red reminded Benny of the Alden's boxcar. Benny knew the boxcar, Grandfather, and their dog, Watch, would all be waiting for them when the children were done returning the seven artifacts for the Reddimus Society. But he missed seeing them. And it had been nice to have Cousin Joe, Cousin Alice, and Soo Lee with them as they traveled through China and Thailand—especially with the archrival Argents constantly trying to throw them off course.

Violet noticed Benny's quietness. As if she knew what he was thinking, she said, "Don't be too homesick, Benny. Cousin Alice told us someone will be waiting for us at our next stop. I wonder who it could be."

The idea that someone familiar would be waiting for them—wherever they were going—

gave Benny a warm feeling of relief. He nodded. "Maybe Grandfather?"

Jessie ruffled Benny's hair. "Maybe! We have plenty of friends and family who might be there to pick us up. Think of it as a surprise!"

Benny imagined Grandfather and Watch waiting for them at the airport when they arrived at their next stop. His worries about the Argents faded.

"I can't wait to see who it is," he said. "Let's think about our clue, so we can find out!"

They all looked at it closely to see if there was a hidden message like the previous clues they had received. Violet noticed the figure of a wiggly snake and a fish among the painted shapes. She pointed at one of the animals.

"That looks like a kangaroo. See the long feet and the tail?" she said. "I learned about this style of painting in art class. It looks like Aboriginal art."

"What's *Aboriginal*?" Benny asked.

"Aboriginal Australians were the first people to live in Australia," Jessie explained. "There are many Aboriginal groups in Australia, like there are many groups of Native Americans in the United States."

"So that means—" Violet began.

"We're going to Australia!" Benny exclaimed. He had learned in school about the animals that live on the continent. Some are so special they can't be found anywhere else in the world. "I want to see kangaroos. And koalas!"

"But where in Australia?" Henry asked. As the oldest, he was not quite as excited as Benny. When he saw the boomerang, he had thought the Aldens might be going to Australia. But he hadn't wanted to say too much around their pilots, Emilio and Mr. Ganert. When the children had been in Thailand, they had figured out one of the pilots was working for the Argents.

The Aldens' friend from the Reddimus Society, Tricia Silverton, had worried someone was giving information to their rivals. That's why she hid all her instructions in riddles and clues. It was like a code only the Aldens could crack. Henry knew they would need to tell their pilots where they were going, but he didn't want to give them any more information than he needed to.

"Isn't Australia an island?" Benny asked.

"Yes, but it's a very big island," Jessie explained. "It's almost the size of the continental United States."

Violet was still looking at the boomerang. It wasn't long before she noticed something.

"Look," she said. "Some of the dots in the pattern have smaller dots inside them."

They all looked closer. Inside some of the red dots were tiny yellow dots. They were hard to see unless the children looked closely.

"Good eyes, Violet," Henry said.

Together, they found all the red dots with yellow centers. Violet drew an invisible line with her finger. The invisible line made letters, which she spelled out loud so she wouldn't forget.

"S...Y...D...N...E...Y," she spelled. "Sydney!"

"Just like connect the dots!" Benny said. "Is Sydney a place in Australia?"

"Not just a place, but one of Australia's most exciting places!" came a jolly voice from behind them. "It's the capital of New South Wales and one of Australia's largest cities."

The Aldens looked up. Emilio walked into the cabin. He and the other pilot, Mr. Ganert, took turns flying the plane.

"Ready for a great joke about Australia?" Emilio asked.

"Not right now," Henry said politely. In the beginning, he had enjoyed Emilio's silly jokes. But now that they knew Emilio might be working for the Argents, they wondered if maybe his jokes were part of his disguise. "It does look like we're headed to Sydney, though. Is it a long flight from here?"

"Hmm, from here it's about nine hours. I'll tell Mr. Ganert to set a course right away. I'm glad you figured out the clue, even if you all seem very serious right now...We'll save the joke for another time."

Emilio winked before he went back to the cockpit. Benny sighed.

"I kind of wanted to hear the joke," he said.

"I've got a joke that has to do with Australia," Jessie said. "What do you call a lazy baby kangaroo?" She paused and looked at her siblings. "A pouch potato!"

Connecting the Dots

Benny imagined a baby kangaroo lazing about in its mother's pouch, and it made him laugh.

"A pouch potato! That's a good one, Jessie."

The four children were getting used to long flights, so the trip to Australia was not bad at all. Jessie spent the flight reading about Sydney on her laptop. Henry played checkers with Benny while Violet drew dot animals like the ones on the boomerang. She drew animals they had seen in their travels: a camel from Egypt, a giraffe from Kenya, and an elephant from Thailand.

By the time the Reddimus plane began to descend, all four Aldens went to the windows. Sydney looked like a big city, and it stretched right up to the coast. There were many little islands in the bay and a big arched bridge. The children could see boats going back and forth between the ports.

"What's that?" asked Benny, pointing to a building that looked like a white seashell.

"That must be the Sydney Opera House," Jessie exclaimed. "I was reading about it. It's a very famous building where all sorts of performances take place."

"Operas? Like singing?" Benny asked.

"Yes. They also have a ballet, a theater company, and an orchestra."

"It would be so wonderful if we could listen to the orchestra," Violet said as the opera house passed out of sight. The airport came into view, and Mr. Ganert's grumpy voice came over the speakers to tell them they were going to land soon. Henry checked on the three remaining Reddimus boxes. To keep the boxes safe, the Aldens had put one in each of their three remaining camera cases. The fourth case belonged to Violet. But they had used it as a decoy in Thailand to help them figure out if one of their pilots was working for the Argents. Now they had three cases left, one for each Reddimus box.

When the children exited the plane onto the tarmac, they were surprised to see a familiar face waiting for them. It was Grandfather's sister, Great Aunt Jane! She was dressed up in a splendid yellow dress and blue hat. She even had a string of pearls around her neck. She gave them all hugs when they met her.

"My, look at you all in your fancy private jet!" she exclaimed.

"Aunt Jane! It's so good to see you," Jessie said. "You look very fancy yourself! What's the occasion?"

"The four of you, of course. Your grandfather called to chat the other day and told me what you have been up to. Then this morning, I got a call from Mrs. Silverton asking if I had any interest in visiting Australia! She said her granddaughter Tricia believed I was the perfect person to meet you. I couldn't tell you why, but I'm glad to be here! She even booked tickets for the five of us to see the orchestra and tour the Sydney Opera House! That's why I'm all done up like this. It's a very special occasion."

Violet and Benny exchanged looks and jumped with joy. They calmed themselves when Emilio and Mr. Ganert joined them on the tarmac. Henry introduced Aunt Jane but did not say anything about the tour or the orchestra.

"Be sure to call and let us know when you find the next clue," Emilio said. "I'm sure Trudy will be glad to know we're one step closer to returning all the items."

Trudy was Mrs. Silverton's other granddaughter and Tricia's sister. While Tricia secretively left the clues for the Aldens to follow, Trudy was the Silverton the Aldens talked to most. She helped them make travel arrangements.

"Don't dawdle," Mr. Ganert added gruffly.

The Aldens said good-bye to the pilots and went with Aunt Jane to check in with their passports. After that was taken care of, Aunt Jane called a taxi, and the five of them left the airport. Violet was especially glad to see Aunt Jane. She sat next to her in the taxi. When they first met Aunt Jane, she was unfriendly, but as the children spent more time with her, Aunt Jane had grown to like them. After a little while, she mended her relationship with Grandfather and became close to the family again.

Violet told Aunt Jane about their travels so far. Henry, Jessie, and Benny sat with their camera cases on their laps, keeping the precious Reddimus boxes in sight at all times. Even if they had left Emilio and Mr. Ganert back at the airport, their journey to Sydney was probably not a secret by now. Anna Argent, who had been following them all over the world trying to get the Reddimus boxes, could show up when they least expected.

"The opera house is a very special place, but I'm afraid we didn't bring any fancy clothes to wear to the show," Jessie said. "We probably can't go and see the orchestra in our jeans and T-shirts after traveling all over the world in them."

"The opera house doesn't have a formal dress code, but even if they did, your grandfather took care of that as well. He is always thinking, that brother of mine."

They got to the hotel just as the sun began to set. It was a tall building right on the bay, and from their room they could see the lights of the city twinkling off the water. The opera house was lit up with white lights so that it almost glowed.

Laid out on the hotel beds was a dress for Violet, a blouse and some slacks for Jessie, and trousers and dress shirts for the boys. There was even a necktie for Henry. After they were dressed, they all looked at one another.

"Henry looks so handsome," Aunt Jane remarked. "And Benny! Very dapper."

Jessie combed her hair and smoothed her blouse. Dressing up was one of the best parts about going to the orchestra. Once they were all ready to go, Aunt Jane called the front desk to order a taxi. While she was on the phone, Benny turned to Henry.

"What will we do with the Reddimus boxes?" he asked.

"Look," Jessie said, pointing to a metal box in the corner. "Our room has a safe. We can store them there while we're at the opera house."

Henry and Jessie read the instructions to open the safe. They placed the Reddimus boxes inside and locked the door. There was no way Anna Argent or the other Argents could get to them now. After a few minutes, Aunt Jane told them it was time to go, and they all went down to the hotel lobby and met their taxi.

By the time they arrived at the opera house, the sky was dark enough that all the city lights seemed more fantastic than ever. The sail-shaped structures of the opera house soared over their heads. All around them, people admired the building from the outside, taking photos with their cell phones and cameras.

"The tour is first. Then we'll get something to eat before we listen to the orchestra," Aunt Jane said. "There are all kinds of venues inside, not just theaters. They have restaurants too!"

Benny's stomach growled.

"I love the Sydney Opera House!" he declared.

Riddle behind the Scenes

The opera house tour was led by an energetic young man with curly black hair. The Aldens walked along with the rest of the tour group. They got to see inside the main concert hall, where the orchestra was preparing for the evening's performance. They even got to see the greenroom, where the theater staff and performers gathered before and after shows. Their guide answered everyone's questions with precise detail.

"How many tiles are there on the roof?" asked one guest.

"There are one million fifty-six thousand and six sail tiles!" replied the guide with a big grin.

"He probably gets asked that a lot," Violet said.

She had seen the tiles on the roof from outside and had wondered how many there were too.

"It would take a long time to count them all," Benny added. He liked to count, but more than one million tiles would probably make his eyes cross. "How long would it take, Henry?"

"I'm not sure, Benny. Probably a long, long time." Henry seemed distracted.

Benny and the girls paused, letting Aunt Jane and the rest of the tour group move ahead a little way.

"What's wrong, Henry?" Jessie asked quietly.

"I'm just worried because we haven't gotten another clue yet," he said. "Remember when that fake message told us to go to Thailand? We got all the way there before we found out we had been tricked."

"Don't worry, Henry," Violet said. "We are on the right track. Aunt Jane wouldn't have met us here if we weren't."

"And don't forget. We're a step ahead of them now," Jessie added. "We know that one of the pilots is telling Anna Argent where we are—"

"But *they* don't know that *we* know!" finished Benny.

Henry sighed again and nodded, but this time he looked relieved.

"You're right. I hope we get the next clue soon. In the meantime, we should also think of a plan to find out which of the pilots is working for the Argents. If we can figure that out, we can ask the other pilot for help."

"Returning the items would be much easier if we didn't have to worry about this," Jessie agreed. "We will all think. I'm sure that we can come up with a good plan together."

The Aldens rejoined their group and the tour guide took them through many areas of the opera house. Jessie saw many people dressed in jeans and T-shirts, but she was still glad they had gotten the chance to dress up. It was a fun change from the sometimes-rugged traveling they had done.

When the tour ended, the Aldens went with Aunt Jane to their dinner reservation. The restaurant was impressive, with candle-lit tables set under one of the opera house's swooping arches. They could see the night sky through the windows in the ceiling.

Their dinner was served in three courses. The first course was a salad of delicious greens. While the others enjoyed their food, a second waiter with a purple bow tie came up to Jessie and tapped her on the shoulder. She was surprised because she hadn't ordered anything else, but then she noticed his bow tie. Purple was the favorite color of the Reddimus Society.

"I believe this is for you," the waiter said. He slipped a little white envelope out of his sleeve and onto the table. "*Bon appétit.*"

Jessie looked at the envelope. It was plain except for the Reddimus logo on one side, an *R* in a circle made of swirls. A drawing of a smart-looking owl sat on top of the *R*. The Aldens had grown to love seeing the Reddimus owl, and it was a good sign to see it printed on the envelope. After the waiter left, Jessie showed the envelope to Henry with a smile. It had to be the clue they were waiting for.

"See? We're on the right track after all," she said.

"I'm glad," said Henry.

Riddle behind the Scenes

"Open it up!" Benny exclaimed. "Let's see what it says!"

Jessie unfolded the note and gave it to Violet, who read it quietly to the others:

> *I am known throughout the world.*
> *I have sails, but I do not sail the sea.*
> *I am filled with song, though I do not sing.*
> *When was my music first heard?*

"Sails?" Benny repeated. "Maybe we're looking for some kind of ship or boat."

"That's a good guess, Benny," Violet agreed. "Australia is an island, and there are lots of ships around. But the riddle said *I do not sail the sea.* What kind of boat stays on land?"

Jessie had an idea. She remembered what the opera house looked like when they had seen it from the outside. "Do you remember what the tour guide said about the tiles on the roof?" she asked. "He said they were called *sail tiles.*"

"The opera house does look like it has sails," Violet said.

"I think it looks more like a seashell," Benny said. "But I guess it could look like sails on a boat too. It's big and white and sort of triangle shaped. And I don't think it can go out to sea."

"*I am filled with song, though I do not sing,*" Henry repeated from the riddle, thinking. "There are all sorts of musical performances that happen here. Like the orchestra and the opera."

"So the riddle is talking about the opera house itself!" Jessie exclaimed. "In that case, all we need to do is find out when the opera house's music was first heard."

"I'm sure somebody here can tell us," Henry said.

"Should we go find someone right now?" asked Violet, remembering how Henry had been worried during the tour.

Henry shook his head.

"No," he said. "I'm sure now that we're on the right track. I feel better about sightseeing. Let's find the tour guide and ask him our question after we enjoy the concert."

They finished their delicious dinner, and then Aunt Jane gave the children their tickets for the concert hall. One at a time, they handed their tickets to the usher standing at the door. Then the usher showed them all to their seats. The hall was large and tall, colored in golds and reds. They had a grand view of the stage, where the Sydney Symphony Orchestra players were just taking their seats. All of the musicians were dressed in fancy black-and-white tuxedos and gowns.

"Here is something interesting to know about the orchestra," Aunt Jane said as the musicians tuned their instruments. "When you go to an energetic rock-and-roll concert, you often applaud after each song to show that you're having a good time. But at the symphony, sometimes a piece of music has a quiet ending. If it's quiet, it's okay to not clap right away, or at all. The orchestra wants you to *feel* the music."

Benny wasn't sure what Aunt Jane was talking about until the music started. Then he understood. Sometimes one of the orchestra's pieces would end with a very exciting, loud ending, and everyone in the hall would applaud. But other pieces would end very quietly and slowly, and the hall would be filled with a lovely silence afterward. Either way, the music was wonderfully performed, and the children felt all kinds of emotions while they listened. At the end, everyone stood up and applauded and cheered happily.

"What a performance!" Aunt Jane said once they were outside of the hall. The main lobby where they stood was full of people talking about the concert. "Did you all enjoy it?" she asked.

"Every moment!" said Violet.

"Do you think someone here will know when the opera house was built?" Benny asked. He had enjoyed the concert too, but he was also eager to solve the riddle. "It might be hard to find our tour guide from before with all these people," Jessie said. "Maybe we can find someone else who knows the opera house well."

"How about that young woman?" Aunt Jane suggested, pointing. There was an usher standing near one of the hall doors, but because the concert was over, she was not helping people find their seats. "Ushers must learn all sorts of things about the places where they work. It's part of their job to help visitors when they have questions. I'll bet she knows a lot about the opera house."

"Yes, let's ask her," Jessie said.

"In the meantime, I'll go to the front desk and see if I can get in touch with any of the tour guides," Aunt Jane said. "I'll let you know what I find. Don't go too far, or I'll never find you in this crowd!"

Aunt Jane waved and went to do as she had said. The usher looked pleased to have someone to talk to when they approached. She was just a little older than Henry, dressed in a crisp usher's uniform.

"Hello!" she said. "Did you all enjoy the concert?"

"Very much," said Henry.

"Can you tell us when the opera house was built?" Benny asked.

The usher tapped her chin.

"Hmm," she said. "If I remember correctly, it was built between the years 1959 and 1973. It takes a long time to construct something so big and complex."

This wasn't the answer Benny had been hoping for. The code for the box had to be four digits. While they thought about the puzzle, a man who

had been looking at some of the art hanging in the lobby wandered closer. He seemed very interested in looking at a painting close to where Benny was standing.

"It probably took so long to build because of all those sail tiles," Benny said quietly. "But we can only use four numbers for the code. Do we use 1959 or 1973?"

"Maybe we've misunderstood the riddle," Jessie suggested. She took it out of her pocket and read it again.

> *I am known throughout the world.*
> *I have sails, but I do not sail the sea.*
> *I am filled with song, though I do not sing.*
> *When was my music first heard?*

"Oh!" the usher exclaimed after she read the riddle. "Although construction took almost fifteen years, music wasn't heard here until the opera house officially opened in 1973," she said loudly. She was having a good time helping them.

"1973," Henry repeated to himself so that he

would remember. "Thank you very much!"

Aunt Jane came back and found the children sitting on a bench in the lobby.

"I didn't find much. All the tour guides are on tours. Can you imagine that?" said Aunt Jane.

"That's fine," said Jessie. "We found out the year from the usher!"

Aunt Jane's face brightened with a smile. "Oh? Good! By the way, who was that man?"

Henry looked over his shoulder, back toward where they had been talking with the usher.

"What man?" he asked.

Benny tugged Henry's sleeve. "There was a man standing by me. He was looking at the paintings, but I think he was trying to hear us too. He moved closer when Jessie read the riddle." Benny looked toward where the man had been standing, but he was gone.

"Hmm, that sounds suspicious," Aunt Jane said. "The Reddimus boxes are back at the hotel, aren't they?"

"Yes," Jessie said. "But if the man was listening and heard us figure out the year the opera house opened, he knows the code to the Reddimus box."

"This could be bad," Henry said, standing up. "We should get back to the hotel right away!"

The Coin in the Box

When they returned to their hotel room, Aunt Jane helped the children make sure nothing in the room had been touched since they left. Everything seemed to be in its rightful place. The safe was closed, and nothing looked like it had been moved. If Anna or one of the other Argents had been in the room looking for the Reddimus boxes, they had not left any trace.

"Even still, I'll go down to the front desk and see if the staff has noticed anything strange going on," Aunt Jane said. "You four stay in the room, and I'll let you know what I find out."

"Thank you!" said Jessie.

After Aunt Jane left, Henry opened the safe.

The three Reddimus boxes were waiting inside. Each one had a different pattern of dots. The dots represented the order the boxes were supposed to be delivered in. They took out the one marked with five dots.

"I'm glad it's still here," said Henry. "Let's open it up and figure out where we're supposed to take it."

Jessie nodded in agreement. "If the Argents know the code, the sooner we return it, the better."

Henry set the wooden box on one of the hotel beds and unlatched it. Inside was another case with a ten-digit keypad on it. Everyone gathered around.

"1973," Benny reminded Henry. He was excited to see inside.

Henry typed in the code, and the box clicked open. Inside was a silver coin, about an inch and a half in diameter. Instead of being solid like other big coins they had seen, this one had a hole in the center. It looked as though the middle had been punched out.

"It looks like a coin, but it's not like any I've ever seen," Violet said.

Benny added, "I wonder if it's worth a lot of money!"

"It may be," Henry said. He was interested in collecting things, like coins and stamps. "Coins can be worth money because of the materials they are made of, like silver or gold. They can also be valuable if there aren't many of them."

"It looks like there's writing on it," Violet said. "What does it say?"

The Coin in the Box

Henry handed the coin to Violet, who squinted at the small words on the coin. "*Dei Gratia Carolus III*," she read. "And there's a date: 1773."

"That would be the year it was minted," Henry said. "It is really strange, though. I think I've seen those words on a different coin before, but I've never seen a coin this big with a hole in it."

Jessie took her laptop out of her backpack. "Let's look it up!" she said as she typed out the words from the coin. The others gathered around to look. The words *Dei Gratia Carolus III* brought up many pictures of silver coins. The coins on the Internet looked like the one in the box, but none of the coins they could find online had holes in the middle.

"It says these are Spanish silver dollars," Jessie said. "They are also called pieces of eight because they were worth eight reales. A real is another kind of Spanish coin...But either way, I don't see any with holes."

"The hole must be what makes it important," Violet suggested. "Maybe we'll have to wait for the next clue before we learn more about the coin."

They all agreed and returned the coin to its box

and locked it. Henry put all three boxes back in the safe.

"It's getting late. I'll call Emilio and Mr. Ganert and let them know we're spending the night here," he said. "Tomorrow maybe we'll have a clue for where we're going next."

While Henry called Emilio, Aunt Jane returned. Jessie and Benny got up to help her and hold the door because Aunt Jane's arms were full with a wrapped package.

"The front desk said there were two people here asking about four children, a young man and a blond woman with a ponytail," Aunt Jane said. "It's against the hotel's policy to share room numbers of guests, so the two went away."

"That sounds like Anna Argent and the man eavesdropping on us at the opera house," Jessie said.

"So Anna is here in Sydney after all!" Violet exclaimed. "What will we do?"

Henry stayed calm. "Same thing as we have been doing: return the artifacts and keep them out of the Argent's hands," he said. "Now that we know

Anna has followed us here, we just have to be as careful and alert as ever."

Henry was right. Anna had been behind them every step of the way until now and they had still been successful. There was nothing to do except keep moving forward with the Reddimus Society's mission.

"What's with the package?" Benny asked. Aunt Jane looked at the wrapped box she had carried up from the lobby.

"Oh, right. After the front desk clerk told me about those two suspicious characters, he remembered that a courier had dropped this off. Imagine my disappointment when I saw it was addressed to the four of you and not to me!" She winked and Benny giggled. "Go on. Let's see what's inside."

Inside the package were four stuffed animals. They were kangaroos, downy and plush with shining glass eyes. They were light brown with dark-colored paws. Two had pouches, and two had no pouches. Violet took one with a pouch and gave it a hug to see how soft it was. It was very soft, but something crinkled when she hugged it.

She looked and found a paper note in the stuffed animal's pouch.

"What have you got there, Violet?" Aunt Jane asked.

"*Please visit us at our island home, and we will help you on your way,*" Violet read. "Our next clue!"

"Isn't all of Australia an island?" Benny asked. "And a bunch of littler islands. How will we know where we're supposed to visit?"

"Good question," Jessie said.

"When I was in the lobby, I saw some flyers for different sightseeing places in Australia," said Aunt Jane. "I believe one had kangaroos on it. You might go down and take a look."

Aunt Jane's suggestion sounded like a good one, so down to the lobby they went. Near the information desk there was a stand with dozens of flyers advertising all kinds of tourist and sightseeing activities. There were flyers about cruises, outback adventures, and snorkeling trips to the Great Barrier Reef.

"Half of these have pictures of kangaroos on them!" said Benny. "How will we know which one is right?"

"When people think of Australia, I guess they think of kangaroos," Jessie agreed. "Maybe this is a dead end."

"Wait, look at this one," Violet said. She had been studying the advertisement rack, looking at each flyer one at a time. She pulled one out and showed the others. "It's a place called Kangaroo Island!"

The flyer had a photo of four kangaroos on the front, two with pouches and two without. They looked just like the stuffed animals in the package. They brought the flyer back to their room and Benny arranged the stuffed animals on the bed so they matched the photo on the flyer.

"It says here that Kangaroo Island is a wildlife preserve," Violet said, reading the flyer while Jessie looked up Kangaroo Island on the Internet. "We can reach it by ferry from a place called Adelaide."

"It looks like Adelaide is a two-hour flight from here, in South Australia," Jessie said. "We can make it there tomorrow if we take the Reddimus jet."

Henry yawned and nodded.

"Then we should get to bed and rest up. Tomorrow we're going to Kangaroo Island," he said.

They all had a good sleep. Benny hugged his cozy stuffed kangaroo all night long. In the morning, they had a light breakfast and went to the airport. Aunt Jane was particularly interested in looking inside the Reddimus jet, which she had seen only from the outside. The Aldens reminded her that one of the pilots was an Argent spy.

"Don't you worry," Aunt Jane said. "I'm very good at keeping secrets! Maybe that's what Tricia Silverton meant when she told her grandmother I was perfect for this trip."

Emilio looked happy to see the Aldens, while Mr. Ganert simply looked relieved that they had returned with the next destination in mind.

"Our next stop is Adelaide," Henry told the pilots. He didn't say anything about Kangaroo Island.

"Adelaide!" said Emilio. "Very good. All aboard!"

The flight was a quick one compared with others they had taken. It seemed like hardly the blink of an eye before Mr. Ganert brought the plane down to the Adelaide airport. Aunt Jane suggested that they leave their stuffed kangaroos on the plane so they wouldn't get lost. When they were ready to go,

Mr. Ganert and Emilio stood near the door to see them off.

"Where are you headed next?" Emilio asked while Henry, Jessie, and Benny put their camera cases around their necks. The Reddimus boxes were safe inside the camera cases, and it was easy to keep a close eye on them around the two pilots. Thinking about how to reply to Emilio's question, Benny and Violet looked at Jessie. "We're not quite sure yet," she said. "We hope to find out the next clue here in Adelaide."

Mr. Ganert frowned. "We've flown all the way here, and you don't even know where you're going next? Surely you have some idea."

"When they have an idea, they'll be certain to tell you," Aunt Jane said.

"Necessarily," Mr. Ganert grumped, turning away and going back to the cockpit. "Or else you'll have to learn to fly this plane yourselves!"

"Don't worry about Mr. Ganert," Emilio said. "He's just eager to return the Reddimus items, I'm sure. Enjoy yourselves in Adelaide and let us know when you hear about the next clue."

The Shackleton Sabotage

"We will. Thank you, Emilio," Henry said.

Adelaide was smaller than Sydney but no less exciting. Aunt Jane showed the children how to use the bus map at the station. Even though she hadn't been to Adelaide, she was good at reading maps, and soon enough they had a plan. They would ride a bus two hours to Cape Jervis, where they could catch the ferry to Kangaroo Island. The buses were well organized and easy to find, so soon enough they were watching the palm trees pass by from their bus seats.

The city faded away as the bus took them into the countryside of South Australia. The bus route went along the coast, where the ocean was so bright and clear they could see the seaweed and white sand below. Benny imagined all the fish and other animals that lived out there.

Cape Jervis was not really a town. It was more of a parking lot with a pier and some docks. The ferry that would take them to Kangaroo Island was parked at one of the docks. The Aldens thanked the bus driver and walked toward the dock. There were many tourists getting ready to board the ferry.

Everyone was excited to get to Kangaroo Island.

"No sign of Anna Argent," Henry said, relieved. "Wouldn't it be nice to have one adventure without her!"

Aunt Jane chuckled. "But how else would that Anna Argent get a chance to travel the world?" she said. "If she weren't trying to steal the Reddimus boxes, she might be awfully bored!"

The children laughed. It was funny to imagine Anna Argent bored at home. As long as Anna didn't get away with stealing the artifacts, maybe it was just fine that she was getting to see all the fun and interesting places the Aldens were seeing.

Aunt Jane bought tickets for the ferry and they boarded. It was a large boat, big enough for all the tourists who were headed to Kangaroo Island. It was so big that it even had a place for some of the tourists' cars, right on the boat. Benny watched the waves below the ferry as it left Cape Jervis. The breeze coming from the ocean was fresh and cool.

"What do you think, Benny?" Jessie asked. "How does the ferry compare to the other kinds of transportation we've taken?"

"I liked the train a lot," said Benny. "It reminded me of our boxcar. But I also like flying in the plane."

"What about riding the camels in Egypt?" Violet asked.

Benny shook his head. "They're all great. I can't decide."

"Look, up there," Henry said, pointing. There was an island in the distance. "That must be it."

"I can't wait to see some kangaroos!" Benny said.

CHAPTER 4

A Curious Acrostic

Kangaroo Island wasn't very large, but there was plenty to see and do. Where the ferry docked, signs advertised several different wildlife sanctuaries, along with shuttles to the hotels and resorts on the island.

"My goodness," exclaimed Aunt Jane. "I didn't realize there would be so many places to visit on one little island. How will you know which place is the right one?"

At first, Jessie wasn't sure either. The five of them looked around for another clue that might help them on their way. Then Jessie saw a young woman in a tour guide's outfit wearing a purple bandanna around her neck.

"Excuse me," Jessie said. "Are you...are you a friend of owls?"

The woman laughed.

"Why, yes I am!" she said. "Hoot, hoot! You must be the Aldens. Jessie, is it? And you must be Henry, Violet, and Benny! I'm Laura. Tricia let me know you were coming."

"Friend of owls?" Aunt Jane asked.

"It's kind of an inside joke," Violet explained.

Friends of owls was a secret greeting among the Reddimus Society—or, at least, that's what the Aldens had been told. Most people thought it was a silly thing to say, but it had helped the Aldens find their Reddimus contacts, so Violet was very glad for it. Aunt Jane chuckled to herself as they followed Laura to her jeep.

"Tricia asked me to take the four of you to the Wildlife Sanctuary here on Kangaroo Island. I work there part-time as a guide when I'm not working here. I'm a naturalist," Laura explained.

"Does a naturalist's job have to do with nature?" Violet asked.

"Yes, it does! I study animals in nature to

understand their needs and behaviors. Then I use that information to help humans and animals live better together. I've been studying the wallabies out here on Kangaroo Island."

"What's a wallaby?" Benny asked.

"Oh, it's like a small kangaroo! They're very cute. I'm sure we'll see some when we reach the sanctuary."

It was a short drive to the sanctuary. When they arrived, Laura parked her jeep and showed them to the visitor center. There were all kinds of maps and informational signs on the walls. There was even a little gift shop with a sign that said the money went to help improve the sanctuary and help it care for the animals.

"I just need to check in, and then we'll go on the tour," Laura said. "Give me one moment."

While Laura went to take care of checking in, the Aldens looked around the visitor center. Jessie walked through the gift shop and looked at the keychains and travel accessories. Benny and Violet took a look at the pictures of the Australian wildlife on the signs. Many of the Australian animals had long names that were hard to read. Violet helped Benny sound out the letters.

"P-L-A-T-Y-P-U-S," he read. "Platypus! I've seen pictures of those in books. They're from Australia too?"

The platypus in the picture was a funny animal that looked like the cross between a beaver and a duck. It had a furry body and tail, but on its face was a flat beak. It looked almost like a made-up animal, but there was a photograph of a real one next to the picture.

"Australia has many unique animals," Laura said. She had come back and was holding five visitor badges on lanyards. "There's a special word for animals that only come from one place. We call them endemic to that place."

"Endemic," Violet repeated. "So kangaroos are endemic to Australia?"

"Exactly!"

"Platypuses are endemic to Australia too!" Benny said. He thought about some of the other animals they had seen. "We saw elephants in Thailand, but elephants also live in Africa," he said. "So they are not endemic because they come from more than one place."

"You've got it, Benny," Laura said. "Now, here are your tour badges. Let's go see the wildlife sanctuary!"

They followed Laura through the visitor center and out the rear exit. The area behind the visitor center looked like a park, with open grassy spaces and other areas that were shaded with trees. But the best part about the park were the dozen kangaroos that were hopping and foraging in the sanctuary. Some played with each other and others lounged in the shade.

"They're so fluffy!" said Jessie. "Look at the little ones!"

"Some of the little ones aren't kangaroos but wallabies," Laura said. "You can tell by looking closely at their forearms. A young kangaroo might be the same size as a wallaby, but its forearms are longer. Here, you can feed them!"

Laura gave them each a plastic bag full of food pellets. The kangaroos and wallabies were not frightened of humans. In fact, some of them hopped right up and ate pellets out of Benny's and Violet's hands. Aunt Jane fed some of the wallabies too.

"It reminds me of feeding the goats back on the farm," she said wistfully. "Oh, look at the little one in the pouch!"

One of the kangaroos had a baby in its pouch. The baby kangaroo's head poked out as he looked around.

"It looks cozy in there," said Benny.

"It's also much safer," Laura said. "Baby kangaroos—we call them joeys—are very, very small when they're born. They stay safe and grow in their mothers' pouches. That way the mother can take the baby wherever she goes, and she doesn't have to worry about predators."

Jessie listened to Laura and looked down at her camera case, where the coin was. The camera case was good, but she wished she had something even safer. The Argents were still following them, and they might know the code to the box. It seemed like if they let their guard down even once, the artifact might be stolen. What if she accidentally set the camera case down and forgot it, even for a minute? Jessie sighed, thinking how nice it would be to have a pouch like the kangaroo. Then she could keep the artifact with her all the time.

After they fed the kangaroos, Laura showed them a trail that went through the park. On the other side of some of the trees was another building that had an attached outdoor pen.

"The sanctuary is sort of like a zoo," Benny said.

"It is, a bit," Laura agreed. "Wildlife sanctuaries are places where injured or endangered animals can go to be treated for medical conditions. Sometimes animals that are injured are unable to go back into the wild, so they live here where we can help take care of them. Many zoos are like that too."

Laura showed them into the pen. The trees in the pen were very green and had a wonderful, minty smell.

"What kind of trees are these?" Henry asked. "They smell great."

"These are eucalyptus trees. Eucalyptus oil is used in many soaps and balms because of that wonderful smell. Eucalyptus is also the food of one of Australia's most famous animals—" Laura pointed up into the trees where a gray, furry animal was climbing.

"A koala!" Benny exclaimed.

"That's Sam, our koala," Laura said. "I'll try to get him down so you can meet him."

Sam the koala seemed happy to see Laura, probably because she had an apple slice for him in her pocket. He climbed down from his tree and onto Laura's arm and shoulder. The Aldens took turns petting him while he ate his apple snack. Aunt Jane even took a photo of him with her phone.

"It looks just like your grandfather when he was a baby," she explained. "I'll send him a photo of it later!"

They all laughed at the thought. Laura put Sam back in his tree when her radio chirped.

"This is Laura, over," she said.

"This is the front gate," said the voice over the radio. "Are you with the Alden children? We just received some mail for them. Over."

"Yes, I'm with them. Will you have it sent to the visitor center? We'll return right away. Over and out!" Laura put her radio back on her belt.

"You weren't expecting any mail, were you?" asked Aunt Jane.

"Yes and no," Henry said. "We are waiting for some clues from Tricia, but we didn't know when they would come."

"Then let's get back to the visitor center and see what's waiting for us!"

Back at the visitor center, the clerk handed Henry the envelope. He read it out loud:

Unique to us, and in this order,
An acrostic to help you find what you need.
He takes care of one of these:
NUMBAT
ECHIDNA
DINGO
WALLABY
EMU
BILBY
BANDICOOT

"What are all those words?" Benny asked. "Are they names? They're tricky!"

"Look, one says wallaby," Violet pointed out. "That's one of the animals we saw on the tour."

"Maybe the other words are also animals," Henry said. "Benny, did you see any of these words while you were looking at the animal pictures here?"

Benny took the note and went to the signs where he had been looking at pictures of animals. He compared the words in the note with the words on the signs.

"Yes, look! Here's one that says echidna. And this one says emu! It's a big bird like an ostrich!"

One by one, they were able to find the animal names on the signs.

"At least now we know they are all animals," Jessie said.

"Unique to us," Benny repeated, thinking about what it could mean. Then he remembered the word they had learned. "Do you think the part that says *unique to us* means the same thing as *endemic*?"

Sure enough, the signs said each animal was endemic to Australia.

"Good thinking, Benny," Henry said.

"But we still don't know what the message means," Violet added. "There's a word in the riddle I don't know. What's an acrostic?"

"An acrostic is a type of puzzle where the first letter of each word spells out a different word," Aunt Jane said. She had been following along and listening to the children as they worked through the riddle.

Jessie snapped her fingers. "Oh, right! I remember now. In school, we did acrostics of our names. We would write the letters of our names on the left side of a sheet of paper. Then we would use those letters to spell words that described us! I'll show you. We'll use Benny's name."

Jessie took out her notebook and a pencil. First she wrote Benny's name on the left. Then they took turns thinking of words that described Benny:

BRILLIANT

ENERGETIC

NICE

NIFTY

YOUTHFUL

"I am very brilliant!" Benny said, putting his hands on his hips. "Brilliant, energetic, nice, nifty, and youthful...Benny!"

They laughed. Now that they understood acrostics, they looked at the clue again. It was easier to understand once they knew what they were looking for. The animal names were all lined up:

> NUMBAT
>
> ECHIDNA
>
> DINGO
>
> WALLABY
>
> EMU
>
> BILBY
>
> BANDICOOT

"The names of the animals spell out NEDWEBB," Violet said. "Ned is a name. Maybe we're looking for someone named Ned Webb?"

"Someone who takes care of one of these animals," Benny agreed. "Maybe someone like Laura!"

Henry nodded. "But where should we look?

Australia probably has many wildlife sanctuaries. There are a few just on Kangaroo Island, not to mention the rest of Australia."

"Let's ask Laura if she's heard of Ned Webb," Aunt Jane suggested. "If he is a naturalist like her, then maybe she's heard his name before."

They found Laura and asked her if she knew of anyone named Ned Webb.

"I do know a Dr. Webb, in fact," Laura said. "He runs a dingo sanctuary just outside of Melbourne. We've worked together before. He is a very... unique...man!"

Laura didn't say what made Dr. Webb so unique, but she did know where the dingo sanctuary was. She found the address in her files and told Jessie, who wrote it down in her spiral-bound notebook.

"What's a dingo?" Benny asked. "Is it like a kangaroo or a wallaby?"

"Oh, no," Laura said. "Dingoes are wild dogs. There were many of them for a long time, but now they are a vulnerable species. That's why people like Dr. Webb have sanctuaries for them."

"Is Melbourne far from here?" asked Henry.

"It's in Victoria. Closer than Sydney," Aunt Jane said. "We could still arrive today."

"Wahoo!" cheered Benny. "Let's go!"

"Just a minute. I want to buy something before we go," Jessie said. She nodded toward the gift shop, remembering something she had seen. Meeting the kangaroos had given her an idea.

After Jessie stopped at the gift shop, they thanked Laura for her help and hurried to catch the ferry back to Cape Jervis. While they were on the ferry, Jessie called Trudy to tell her they had found the owner of the fifth Reddimus artifact. Trudy didn't pick up the phone, so Jessie left a message. The time difference between Australia and the United States was big, so Trudy was probably asleep. She wouldn't get the message until she woke up.

When they got off the ferry, the Aldens caught their bus and were headed back to the Adelaide airport. Emilio and Mr. Ganert were waiting for them. Both looked eager to know where they were going next.

"Victoria," Henry said. He did not tell them the address, though. The Aldens had agreed on the bus that they would go to the dingo sanctuary on their own. What a relief it would be if they could return the coin without running into Anna Argent!

They went up the stairs to the plane with Emilio and Mr. Ganert.

"Anywhere in particular in Victoria?" Emilio asked. "It's a large state..."

"I think Melbourne will be fine," Henry said. "We'll have a lot of options for transportation from there."

"Still not sure where the box is going, eh?" Mr. Ganert asked. He sounded annoyed. "I knew it was silly to trust this delivery to children."

"Now, now, that's not fair," said Emilio. "These riddles Tricia Silverton has left are clever. I don't know that you or I could do any better!" Then to the Aldens, he said, "Just let us know how we can help, all right?"

"Yes, thank you," Jessie said. She took her hand off the handrail to close her notebook, but... "Oh—!"

Henry and Violet caught Jessie's arms as she accidentally tripped on the top step. She caught the handrail but dropped her notebook. It fell open in front of Emilio and Mr. Ganert, still open to the page with the address of Ned Webb's dingo sanctuary!

"Are you okay?" Emilio asked. He picked up the notebook and handed to her. "Here you go."

"Yes, I'm fine," Jessie said, closing the notebook and holding it firmly. Her heart was beating fast. Had they seen the address? She glanced at Henry and Violet as they took their seats in the cabin. Mr. Ganert said nothing before ducking into the cockpit. Emilio whistled to himself and gave them a little salute.

"See you in Melbourne," he said.

After both pilots were in the cockpit preparing for takeoff, Jessie let out a little sigh.

"I can't believe I dropped the notebook!" she said.

"It's okay," Aunt Jane assured her. "I would rather you dropped the notebook than fell down the stairs and got hurt. It will be fine."

"Aunt Jane's right," Henry agreed. "Remember? This wouldn't be the first time they've known where we were going."

Jessie took a few breaths and calmed herself

down. Henry was right. They already knew Anna Argent had followed them to Sydney. It seemed like only a matter of time before she showed up. That was the whole reason Jessie was working on a backup plan of her own. She relaxed as the jet took off, launching into the air.

"Well, I just hope Anna likes dingoes," she said.

CHAPTER

Dingoes on the Loose!

When they reached Melbourne, the Aldens found a bus that would take them to the Webb Dingo Sanctuary. Emilio suggested that they rent a car and offered to drive. But Henry insisted they had enjoyed traveling by bus from Adelaide. Emilio did not argue and instead wished them safe travels.

It was true that traveling by bus was fun. The seats were large and comfortable, and the windows were big, which made watching the landscape easy. The bus took them north from Melbourne. The ride was a couple of hours, so they had plenty of time to tell Aunt Jane more about their adventures. Even though they were nervous that their pilots had seen the address and that the Argents might follow them, Aunt Jane didn't seem worried. She asked questions about their travels and wanted to hear every last detail. When the bus neared their stop, they had almost forgotten about their worries.

"Here we are. This is it," Aunt Jane said, looking at the street signs and comparing them to the bus map she had taken from the station. "Time for us to get off."

They exited the bus and looked around. They stood on a quiet road bordered on one side with a line of trees. A sign for the Webb Dingo Sanctuary was across the road. They had made it!

They followed a dirt road up to a ranch home surrounded by trees. They could hear barks and playful yips coming from around the back of the ranch, where they could see a fenced-in backyard. Benny wanted to take a look, but Aunt Jane reminded him it wasn't polite to go peeking into other people's property. Instead they went to the front porch, where there was a door into a visitor office. It reminded Jessie a little bit of the friendly veterinarian clinic they took Watch to for his yearly checkups. A white cockatoo was sitting on a perch on the front desk. He whistled and said, "Hello!" when they walked in.

"Hello!" Henry greeted. The woman at the desk smiled.

"Hello, did you have an appointment?" she asked. "I'm Dr. Webb's assistant."

"Hello!" said the cockatoo again. Benny giggled.

"No, we don't have an appointment," Henry replied. "But we were hoping to speak with Dr. Webb. Is he available?"

"I think he's out back feeding the pups," said the woman. "I'll go check. Please have a seat and make yourselves at home."

While the woman went to find Dr. Webb, Benny and Violet played with the cockatoo. He said other things besides "Hello." He also said "Snack time!" and mimicked the sound of a dingo barking. On the walls of the lobby were many photographs of dingoes. Some were puppies. Others had casts on their legs or bandages.

"This must be where people take dingoes if they find them hurt," Jessie said. "Look, here's a newspaper article. It says Dr. Webb took care of a dingo after it was hit by a car."

"It's good that the wild animals have someone to take care of them when they need help," Henry said. Then Dr. Webb's assistant came back into the room.

"Dr. Webb can see you in the yard," she said with a friendly smile. "Are any of you allergic to dogs?"

"Nope," Benny said as they followed her down a hallway to the back of the ranch. "We have a dog back home in the United States. His name is Watch."

"What a wonderful name," said the assistant. "Is he a good watchdog?"

"Yes!" Benny said excitedly.

They all chuckled. The hallway took them through some indoor kennels. It ended at a doorway that went out into the backyard. The yard was large and fenced in. Playing in the yard were many dingoes. They were playing with sticks and rope toys and balls. Most of them were golden and yellow, but a couple were black.

The dingoes barked and yipped when they saw the visitors. Some of the puppies ran up to Dr.

Webb's assistant, and she gave them treats from her pockets.

A man was sitting on the ground near some water dishes that looked like regular dog bowls. He was holding a dingo puppy and brushing its teeth. The puppy didn't seem to like having its teeth brushed. It squirmed around, but the man was patient and gentle. Eventually he finished and let the puppy go. It bounded away to play with its brothers and sisters.

"Oh," said the man, standing up. He came over to meet his visitors. His bottom was still covered in dirt and twigs from the ground. "I didn't see you there! Mimi, I didn't know we had guests!"

"I told you about five minutes ago!" Mimi said. It sounded like she was used to his forgetfulness. "This is Dr. Webb."

"Hello, I'm Henry," Henry said. He also introduced his siblings and Aunt Jane.

"Very nice to meet you all," said Dr. Webb. He adjusted his glasses and looked at the children one at a time. "What can I do for you? Did you come on a school field trip? Would you like to learn about the dingoes?"

"The dingoes are wonderful, but we actually have something else to talk to you about," Jessie said.

"Oh my, it sounds important," said Dr. Webb. "Let's go into my office." The Aldens followed Dr. Webb back inside.

Jessie expected Dr. Webb's office to look like a professor's office or maybe a veterinarian's office. Instead it was cluttered and messy, more like someone's living room. There was a couch that looked like it had been chewed on by a dingo, and books and papers were scattered all about. It did have a desk, though, stacked with folders and books and framed photographs of dingoes.

"Now, what was it you wanted to talk about?" asked Dr. Webb. On cue, Henry took out the Reddimus box that held the coin. He opened the box and showed Dr. Webb. When he saw the coin, Dr. Webb let out a gasp.

"Oh my! Could it be?" he exclaimed. He held up the coin and looked at it through his spectacles. "Holey dollar!"

"Is that like 'holy smokes?'" Benny asked.

"No, no!" explained Dr. Webb. "Holey dollar is what this is! It's a silver dollar with a hole in it. These are very rare. There were only forty thousand made and probably only three hundred left in the world!"

"Maybe you could tell us why it has that hole in it?" Violet asked. "We found out it was a Spanish dollar, but we've never seen one with a hole!"

Dr. Webb nodded enthusiastically. He was grinning ear to ear.

"Oh yes. Certainly. You see, Australia didn't have its own money for a long time. They used the currencies of other countries. But they wanted to have their own. So they ordered Spanish silver dollars and punched holes in them. The outside part with the hole was worth fifteen pence—a pence is kind of like a penny—and the coin that came out of the middle was worth five shillings, which was about twenty-five pence."

"Like a quarter?" Henry asked.

"Yes. Except they don't use shillings anymore, so you'd have to figure in the currency conversion from the time..." Dr. Webb trailed off and adjusted his glasses.

"They made two coins out of one," Henry said thoughtfully. "And I suppose if there was a hole in the middle, the Spanish dollar couldn't be used in Spain any longer."

"Precisely. Of course, this didn't last long. They created the holey dollars in 1813, but in 1825 the British government changed all that..." Dr. Webb trailed off again. "Oh, but that's a story for another time. In any case, this is wonderful. Very wonderful. You see, aside from running the dingo sanctuary, I'm a coin collector. The museum in Sydney asked me to verify this coin was authentic. They shipped it to me, but it went missing in the mail. It's so good to know it's safe and sound."

"We should let you know that someone might try to steal it," Henry said. "There is a group who has been trying to steal all the artifacts we're supposed to return. It's probably a good idea to bring it to the museum as soon as you can."

"No worries, my friend!" said Dr. Webb with a smile. "Out here there's nothing to worry about. The dingoes will bark if they see anything suspicious. Ha ha! They also bark if they see anything fun or exciting! Oh, and some of them bark when they're hungry."

"They're even barking right now," Violet said.

Indeed, the dingoes were barking. It sounded like excitement and fun, the way Watch would bark when he saw Benny pick up his favorite tennis ball. He knew that meant it was time to play.

The sounds of the barking grew fainter, and Violet frowned.

"Doesn't it sound like they're going farther and farther from the yard?" she asked.

Dr. Webb tilted his head.

"Yes, it does, a bit," he said. "Let's go see what's going on out there."

Henry, Violet, Benny, and Aunt Jane went with Dr. Webb out to the yard where they found all the dingoes were running around, *outside* the pen. Someone had opened the gate! Mimi was holding one of the puppies and trying to call the others back to the pen, but the dingoes were having too much fun romping and running beyond the yard. Some of them thought Mimi was playing a game of tag with them. Jessie came out a moment later and gasped at the sight of all the dingoes running loose.

"Dr. Webb!" cried Mimi. "You have to help me call them back! They might listen to you."

Dr. Webb rolled his sleeves up and nodded. He put a finger in his mouth and made a loud whistle. One of the dingoes came running back with his tail wagging, but the others were busy chewing on sticks and rolling in the grass.

"I guess we will have to do this the old-fashioned way! Violet, you and Benny stand near the gate. When the dingoes come back to the yard, open the gate for them, but then close it after so they don't get back out. Henry, Jessie, and I will go chase the others down. Mimi, would you get some of the special treats from inside?"

Mimi went to get the treats while Henry and Jessie trotted out of the pen. At least two dozen dingoes frolicked in the lightly wooded area outside the yard. It looked like all the dingoes were having a great time playing. A couple of dingoes smelled the special treats and ran to Henry and Jessie when they called. After they came back into the yard, Violet and Benny gave them the treats for

being well behaved. Then they carefully latched the gate so they couldn't escape again.

Some of the dingoes were more interested in playing tag with Dr. Webb. They wagged their tails and let him come close, but then they ran away at the last second. Jessie could swear the dingoes had a sense of humor and were having fun teasing them.

Eventually, they managed to corral the dingoes back into the pen. Dr. Webb counted them to make sure every one had been found.

"Sometimes this happens," he admitted. "The gate doesn't latch very well and falls open. The dingoes like to run around outside the yard just because it's a game to them. But I always make sure we have everyone back at the end of the day. I wouldn't want any of the dingoes to run too close to the road. It could be dangerous for them."

All the dingoes had come back, so Mimi locked the gate to make sure it would stay shut.

"But who opened the gate to begin with?" Mimi asked. "When it has come open before, it's been by accident because it wasn't latched all the way. But I know for sure I latched it properly today. It couldn't have opened by accident."

"And look at that," said Benny, pointing down at the path. There was a footprint in the dirt that didn't match the footprints left by the children, Dr. Webb, or Mimi. "Doesn't that look like a sneaker?"

It had taken at least half an hour to find all the dingoes and call them back to the yard. The gate might have been opened so that everyone would be busy finding the dingoes. No one would have been inside to keep an eye on things—including the box.

The Aldens exchanged glances. They knew who might do such a thing: the same person who wore sneakers that matched the footprint by the gate.

"Anna Argent!" they said at the same time.

"Quickly, Dr. Webb," Henry said. "We need to be sure the holey dollar is safe. This might have been a distraction by the people who are trying to steal it!"

"Oh, dear!" said Dr. Webb.

They hurried back to Dr. Webb's office. Inside, it was hard to tell because it had already been very messy, but it looked as if someone had been there.

Some of the books had been knocked off the desk and were on the ground, and the window was open where it had been closed before. Most important, the Reddimus box on the desk was open. There was nothing inside.

"Oh, no!" Dr. Webb exclaimed. "Someone stole the holey dollar!"

CHAPTER

Owls and Penguins

Dr. Webb started searching under all the books and papers and research. Henry, Violet, and Benny tried to help, but there was no sign of the coin. "How will we find her? Anna Argent could have gone anywhere by now," Aunt Jane said. "Has this happened before?"

"Yes, once at Stonehenge," Henry said. "But Anna dropped the artifact by accident, and we were able to get it back. Jessie, aren't you going to help us look?"

Jessie hadn't joined the search, but it wasn't because she was being unhelpful. She smiled and lifted up the hem of her T-shirt. Strapped against her waist was a thin travel wallet. It had been hidden under her shirt before. She unzipped it and reached in. Out came the holey dollar!

"Jessie, you knew?" Benny cried.

"That's my grandniece!" said Aunt Jane.

"I put it in my kangaroo pouch before we went outside," Jessie said with a grin. "I thought the dingoes getting out seemed a little strange—like something Anna Argent might do. So I took the coin with me to be safe. Just like a mother kangaroo!"

The Aldens let out a sigh of relief. Henry laughed and wiped his forehead with the back of his hand. "Good thinking, Jessie," he said.

"What a relief!" said Dr. Webb. He took the coin from Jessie when she handed it to him and put it in his pocket. "You know what? I just remembered something. Come with me."

The children followed Dr. Webb back through the building to the front porch where the mailbox was. Dr. Webb opened the mailbox and took out an envelope.

"This came earlier today. It was addressed to the Aldens. I didn't know who that was, so I left it here for the postal worker to take back to the post office.

But you said your last name is Alden, right? In that case, it's for you."

Jessie accepted the envelope and opened it. Inside were four tickets and a note that said: *Not owls this time, but penguins!*

It was marked with the Reddimus logo and a hand-drawn cartoon of an owl and a penguin. Dr. Webb glimpsed the tickets and his eyes widened.

"Oh! Those look like tickets to the Melbourne Aquarium!" he said. "It's a wonderful aquarium. I imagine you'll enjoy it very much."

"On to our next assignment, I guess!" Henry said. He turned to Dr. Webb. "I don't think Anna Argent will come back for the coin once we're gone. Still it's probably best if you return it to the museum soon."

"Yes, absolutely," agreed Dr. Webb. "I'll keep it safe. Now...which pocket did I put it in again?"

"The left pocket!" Benny said. He had been keeping a close eye on Dr. Webb.

"Oh yes! The left pocket. Left. I'll remember this time."

They said good-bye and thank you and walked

back to the bus stop to wait for the bus. The sun was setting, turning the sky a pretty pink.

"It's getting late," said Violet. "Do you think the aquarium will be open by the time we get back to the city?"

Henry checked his watch. "No, you're right. We'll have to go to the aquarium tomorrow."

"Good, because my feet are tired," agreed Benny.

Jessie took out her cell phone. She didn't have any service. "It doesn't look like we'll be able to get in touch with Trudy tonight to tell her our news," she said.

"I saw a sign for a bed-and-breakfast not too far back down the road," said Aunt Jane. "If you don't mind walking just a little longer, we can head there and stay the night. Then we can go back to Melbourne and the aquarium in the morning."

It wasn't a long walk at all, and by the time they arrived at the quaint two-story home, they were ready for supper and a soft bed. Aunt Jane spoke with the owners and checked them into the rooms upstairs. Jessie called Emilio to explain the situation, and as the sun went down, they settled in for the night.

* * *

The next morning as they waited at the bus stop, Henry was especially cheerful.

"Henry, are you feeling better?" Aunt Jane asked.

"Yes, I'm glad we were able to return the holey dollar," he said. "We only have two more boxes!"

"We'll have the last two returned before we know it," Jessie said, smiling at Benny and Violet.

"I'm excited to see the aquarium," Benny said. "When we were on the boat to Kangaroo Island, I was thinking about all the fish that live out in the ocean. I want to see fish and sharks and whales!"

Henry chuckled. "I'm not sure there will be whales at the aquarium, but I'm sure we'll see plenty of fish."

The aquarium was a short walk from where the bus dropped off the Aldens in Melbourne. The building sat right next to the bay.

Aunt Jane's phone rang, and she answered it.

"Hello? Oh, hello! Children, it's your grandfather. He says hello! Listen, why don't you run ahead and have fun at the aquarium. My feet are tired from walking all around Kangaroo Island and the dingo sanctuary, so I think I'll rest out here for a minute and catch up with my brother."

Aunt Jane looked relieved to sit on a bench near the water, so the children agreed to meet her in a couple of hours and went inside. After they showed their tickets, they explored the aquarium's many tanks of colorful fish. There was even a tank exhibit so large they walked underneath it, in a long, clear hallway that let them look up at the fish swimming over their heads.

"Look, Benny, there's a shark!" Violet said, pointing. There were a few sharks swimming gracefully in the water. They didn't bother the other fish in the aquarium. All the fish seemed to get along with each other.

"It's probably still too small to fit a whale in here," Benny said. But he was happy to see all the fish and even a few sharks. They explored the fish aquariums for a while before seeing what other exhibits were available. One of the exhibits in particular caught Violet's eye.

"Let's go and see the penguins!" she said. There was a big display for the penguin exhibit, with photos of small penguins and one big emperor penguin. Everyone agreed seeing the penguins up close looked fun, so they followed the signs through the aquarium. The air got cooler as they got closer to the exhibit.

"It's getting chilly!" Benny said. "They must keep it cold for the penguins."

Henry nodded. "Most penguins come from cool places. They like it nice and brisk!"

The penguin enclosure was different from the other aquariums. Some of it was underwater, but some of it was above the water. Little penguins jumped off the rocks into the water. The exhibit was made of glass so visitors could see right into the water. Benny and Violet wandered ahead and watched the penguins swim around, darting through bubbles and then popping back up onto the rocks.

"It's almost like they're flying underwater," Violet said.

"Because they can't fly in the air like other birds," Benny added. "I can't pick what would be more fun: to fly through the water or fly through the clouds!"

The next area in the exhibit was for a different kind of penguin. They had fluffy yellow feathers on their faces. Benny laughed. "It looks like the penguin has bushy yellow eyebrows!" he said.

An employee standing near the exhibit heard Benny and smiled. "These are called royal penguins," said the woman. "Do you want to take a guess why they have those funny yellow feathers on their faces?"

Benny thought for a moment.

"I don't know. But it does make them look different!"

"That's exactly right," said the woman. "Those yellow feathers help the penguins recognize each other as the same species, even when they are swimming underwater. They're called crests. Most birds have crests, like cardinals and cockatoos. But there is one species that does not...Do you know what kind?"

The woman looked eagerly at Benny and Violet. Then Violet noticed she was wearing a purple collared shirt.

Violet asked in a whisper, "Could it be...owls?"

The woman nodded. "I have a message for you from Tricia Silverton."

She handed Violet an envelope as Jessie and Henry walked over.

"Thank you very much," Violet said. She put the envelope in her pocket.

They finished looking through the rest of the

penguin exhibit and then went outside to find Aunt Jane. She was reading a book on the bench and looking very happy.

"Did you have a good time?" she asked when she saw them.

"Yes, and we got our next clue," Benny said. "Also, I'm hungry! We left so early to get to the aquarium that we missed breakfast."

"Then we had better find something to eat. It's difficult to think on an empty stomach, isn't it? I hear the aquarium's cafeteria is pretty good. Shall we get brunch there?"

The cafeteria had a good menu, and, even better, an outdoor patio. They found a table with an umbrella and enjoyed croissants and orange juice looking out over the bay. While they ate, Violet opened the envelope. Everyone was eager to hear the clue to their next destination, where they hoped to return the sixth Reddimus artifact.

Inside there was a riddle that Violet read:

I was a rumor for hundreds of years,
And once I was found, I belonged to all.

If you are at my center, no matter where you turn,
You are always facing north.
I am full of birds of black and white, but most
    cannot fly.
The year I was first seen gives you what you need.
Then visit me to return what was taken.

"Black and white birds that can't fly!" Benny exclaimed. "Sounds like penguins!"

"But we're already here in Australia," said Jessic. "Where else do penguins come from?"

Violet remembered what she had read while they had been enjoying the penguin exhibit. "The signs in the exhibit said penguins come from many places: Chile, Argentina, the Galapagos, and near the South Pole," she said.

"South Pole," Henry repeated. "Hmm. Listen to this part of the riddle: *No matter where you turn, / You are always facing north.* There's only one place in the world where that could be true. Sounds like the South Pole to me!"

"Is the South Pole a city?" Benny asked. "Or a country?"

"It's more like a geographic location," Henry said. "But it is on the continent of Antarctica. Different countries have claimed land there, but there are still unclaimed areas."

"That's what the riddle could mean by *And once I was found, I belonged to all*," Jessie said. "Yes, it sounds like the riddle is about Antarctica!"

"Then we just have to find out when it was first seen to get the code to the box," Violet said. "And then we're going to visit!"

"Brrr," Benny said. "I bet it's cold. Do people even live in Antarctica?"

Aunt Jane knew something about that. "Oh, yes, but no one lives there permanently," she explained. "Mostly it's scientists. Some explorers too."

"I wonder what kind of thing could have been stolen from a place like that," Henry said. "If there are explorers there, maybe they found something in their explorations, and that's what's in the box."

"Either way, we'll have to get really warm coats," Benny decided.

They finished their meal and took a taxi back to the airport where they met Emilio and Mr. Ganert at the Reddimus jet. The two were playing chess. Both looked a little bored, but Mr. Ganert looked more annoyed that he was losing.

"Welcome back!" said Emilio. "Is that a clue in your hand there?"

"Yes," Violet said. "We are going to Antarctica next."

Emilio and Mr. Ganert shared matching frowns. Mr. Ganert shook his head.

"The Reddimus jet isn't equipped to fly to Antarctica," he said. "If that is the next destination, you'll have to figure out some other way to get there."

"Not equipped?" Henry asked.

"Mr. Ganert's right," Emilio replied. "It's too small and doesn't have the safety equipment. All flights to Antarctica must be equipped with cold-weather gear."

This information was new to the Aldens. How were they going to get to Antarctica if the Reddimus jet couldn't take them? So far it had been able to take them to every destination hidden in Tricia's clues!

Emilio waved his hand. He wasn't worried.

"I'm sure there is a way," he told them. "We'll leave the four of you alone to figure out what comes next. You're clever kids, and I believe in you."

Emilio and Mr. Ganert went to do an engine check on the plane.

"I didn't know planes needed special equipment to go to Antarctica," Benny said once they were alone.

"It's because it's so cold and far away," Aunt Jane said. "In case of emergencies, it's important that the planes are ready for it."

"You sure know a lot about Antarctica, Aunt Jane," said Henry. A smile had been growing on Aunt Jane's face since they had mentioned Antarctica.

"Children, do you remember how Tricia mentioned I would be the perfect person to meet you for this part of your adventure?"

"Yes! Because you're fun and like going to orchestra concerts!" Benny said.

"And you're good at keeping secrets," Violet added.

Owls and Penguins

"Those things are true, but I think I understand now what she meant. You see, I have an old friend who is a historian. He works at McMurdo Station in Antarctica. Ever since I started traveling, he's been trying to get me to visit him. I never thought I would get the chance."

"Your friend is a historian?" Henry said. "How many historians do you think work in Antarctica? There can't be very many."

"Could he be our contact?" Jessie asked.

Aunt Jane grinned and said, "There's only one way to find out!"

The Mysterious Continent

While Aunt Jane used Jessie's laptop to email her historian friend to ask about the best way to reach Antarctica, the children sat in a circle. Even if they got to Antarctica safely, they had other problems to solve.

"We still have to figure out when Antarctica was first sighted," Jessie said. "That should give us the code to the box. Maybe whatever's inside will give us a clue about where in Antarctica we're supposed to take it."

"And who to give it to," Violet added with a nod.

Aunt Jane handed Jessie the laptop.

"I just got an email from Jasper. He told me the best way to get to Antarctica is from Christchurch,

New Zealand. I'll go tell those pilots about Christchurch. By the time we arrive, maybe we'll have a better idea about where in Antarctica we're headed."

While Aunt Jane went outside to talk to the pilots, Jessie researched Antarctic exploration. After seeing some photos of explorers, Benny looked through some of the closets aboard the plane. There were coats, but nothing as warm and puffy as the ones the explorers were wearing in the pictures. The explorers even wore goggles and face masks to protect them from the freezing temperatures.

"This website says Antarctica's lowest recorded temperature is almost one hundred and thirty degrees below zero," Jessie said. "But it says that around this time of year, the average high is...sixty-five degrees below zero!"

"I can't even imagine how cold that is!" Violet said, rubbing her arms. "Even though it's summer here, I feel cold just thinking about Antarctica. Now I understand why only special planes can fly there."

"I just want to wear a cool pair of goggles,"

Benny said. He wished there were goggles in the Reddimus plane's closets.

"You might get to, Benny. I think we'll need special gear for this trip," Henry said. "Jessie, did you find out about when Antarctica was first sighted?"

"Yes, I just did. It says Antarctica was first sighted in 1820."

Henry took out the Reddimus box that contained the sixth artifact. He let Violet type in the code, and the box clicked open. Inside was an old food tin. In old-fashioned lettering on the cover was the word *Biscuits.*

"This looks like something we'd find in Grandfather's attic," Benny said. "What's inside? It says *Biscuits,* but it doesn't look like more than one biscuit could fit in there."

"These are probably a different kind of biscuit," Jessie said. "If this is what I think it is, then they're more like crackers than the fluffy biscuits Mrs. McGregor makes. I'll show you."

Jessie brought up the web page she had been reading about Antarctic expeditions. She showed the others a picture of a biscuit eaten by explorers. It was flat and looked like a wafer or cracker.

"These biscuits were specially made for explorers who had to survive the climate of the Antarctic," Jessie said. "They weren't very tasty, but they had a special recipe that made them excellent to eat when you needed energy. And because they were flat, the explorers could carry many of them in a small space."

"I wonder why an old biscuit tin could be valuable?" Violet wondered aloud.

"Maybe it's valuable because there aren't very many left," Henry suggested. "Like the holey dollar."

"Even if it is, I don't know how this helps us get to Antarctica." Jessie sighed. "We might be able to find out where it needs to be returned to, but that won't help us get there. I think I'm going to try to give Trudy a call...maybe she'll be up."

The children gathered around Jessie's laptop. They called Trudy on Skype. To their surprise, she answered.

"Jessie!" Trudy exclaimed. "Henry, Violet, and

Benny too! Oh, it's good to see your faces. I'm sorry I wasn't able to return your calls. Things have become very...um...busy over here. How are things going for you all?"

"We returned the fifth artifact to Ned Webb, even though Anna Argent tried to stop us," Jessie said. "And we've opened the box for the sixth artifact. But according to the clue we've gotten, we need to go to—"

"Antarctica!" Trudy finished Jessie's sentence. "Of course. I knew you would be calling about that. Tricia left a message for you. Once you solve the riddle, you should know where to go...Also, I hear you have a very knowledgeable helper!"

"Yes, Aunt Jane knows a lot about Antarctica!" Violet said." She even has a friend who lives there," Benny added.

"Hmm. I have the feeling Tricia knew about that," Trudy said with a little grin. "Now listen and write this down. It's the clue to your destination. Are you ready?"

"We're ready!" Jessie said.

Trudy cleared her throat and recited the riddle.

"*Named for a lieutenant who sailed on the* Terror, *I am in the world's southernmost harbor.* Got it?"

Jessie wrote the riddle down and repeated it back. Trudy nodded.

"That's a pretty short riddle," Jessie said. "Is that why Tricia didn't deliver a written clue this time?"

Trudy's smile faded slightly. "Yes, something has come up. You all know Agent Carter?"

The children nodded. Mr. Carter was an FBI agent and friend of Grandfather's. Last they had spoken to him, he was investigating stolen art from a gallery in Nairobi and a stolen ruby ring from an auction in Paris.

"I just got off the phone with him. He was asking about your recent travels and your contact with Tricia." Trudy took a deep breath. "Apparently a theft took place at a museum in Japan last week."

"Theft? Does Mr. Carter think Tricia had something to do with it?" Jessie asked.

"There is a videotape that shows Tricia speaking to a woman with a blond ponytail," Trudy explained. "The woman is thought to be the one who took the artifact on Thursday night."

"That sounds like Anna Argent!" Henry said. He paused to think. "We were in Thailand last Thursday. Anna must have been in Japan! But it's strange that Tricia would be talking to Anna."

"No way Tricia would help Anna steal!" Benny said.

"I don't know why they were talking," Trudy continued. "But the investigators think Tricia's involved. They also think she might have been the one that sent you off to Thailand."

"But it was the Argents that sent us to Thailand," Jessie said. "Plus, Tricia just helped us *return* another artifact, the holey dollar."

"I know she did," said Trudy with a sigh. "But you also said that Anna tried to steal the coin. The police might think that Tricia told Anna where to go."

"But it wasn't Tricia who led Anna to us. It was one of our pilots!" Jessie exclaimed. Just as Jessie finished her sentence, she heard a click-clack of someone walking up the airplane steps.

Jessie took a deep breath. "Sorry, Trudy. We need to go. If you talk to Tricia, let her know we'll figure out who the spy is as soon as we can."

The Mysterious Continent

"I'll tell her. Good luck in Antarctica," Trudy said, waving good-bye. "Remember to stay warm!" They all waved back.

Just as Jessie was closing her laptop, Aunt Jane, Emilio, and Mr. Ganert came back into the cabin. Mr. Ganert went straight into the cockpit. Emilio paused to say, "Next stop, Christchurch, New Zealand!" before he followed.

A minute later the jet started up, so the children and Aunt Jane took their seats and fastened their seat belts. Since the two pilots were busy in the cockpit, the Aldens didn't have to worry about being overheard, so they filled in Aunt Jane on everything they had learned.

"Sounds like we should get cracking on that riddle," Aunt Jane said after they were finished. "It might help show that Tricia is innocent."

Jessie smiled. It was good to have someone with them to help. She took out the piece of paper and held it out so everyone could see.

"*Sailed on the* Terror makes it sound like the *Terror* is a ship," Henry pointed out. "Jessie, will you look online and see if there are any ships named *Terror* that sailed to Antarctica?"

Jessie did a quick search. "Yep, here it is. There was a ship called the HMS *Terror* that explored Antarctica in 1839. But I don't see a list of lieutenants that were on the ship."

"What about the part about being the world's most southernmost harbor?" asked Aunt Jane. "Although every place in Antarctica is farther south that most of the world, I suppose one of them has to be the farthest!"

Jessie looked that up too. When she read the screen, her face lit up.

"Ah-ha! The world's southernmost harbor is McMurdo Sound. And it says here that McMurdo Sound is named after Lieutenant Archibald McMurdo...of the HMS *Terror*!"

"McMurdo...isn't that where your friend works?" Violet asked, remembering what Aunt Jane had said earlier. "Is McMurdo Station in McMurdo Sound?"

"It is indeed!" said Aunt Jane.

"Tricia was right. You really are perfect!" Benny said.

The Mysterious Continent

Aunt Jane gave him one of her best winks. "In every way!" she said, and they all laughed.

* * *

When the Aldens landed, Aunt Jane exchanged a few emails with her friend Jasper, and before long, she found the right desk to buy the special plane tickets that would get them to Antarctica. After they checked in with their passports, Aunt Jane helped Henry and Jessie read the airport terminal screens to find out where their special plane to Antarctica was waiting.

After a few moments, they found the gate for their plane. Even though it was a special flight, the gate was just like other ones at the airport. Aunt Jane checked them in at the desk, and she made sure their names had been added to the list of passengers.

"Yes, you're all registered and good to go," said the flight attendant. "Oh, I've been told to give you these too." He had a big container waiting behind the desk. Inside, the Aldens found five big parkas and enough goggles, hats, gloves, boots, and snow pants for them all. Benny tried on his goggles first. They covered almost his whole face.

"I'm ready for Antarctica!" he said. Everyone, including the flight attendant, laughed.

They got dressed in their gear and went down to the bus that would take them to the aircraft. Other passengers were waiting on the bus, all with their warm parkas. Most of the passengers looked like scientists and researchers, reading books and wearing parkas with science logos.

Benny watched out the window as the bus slowed.

"Wow! Look at the plane!" he said.

It was a big and gray military plane. Inside, it was nothing like the Reddimus jet. It didn't even have the usual rows of seats. Instead, there were stacks of luggage and equipment in crates, strapped down in the center of the cabin. The seats were along the side of the cabin.

Once the plane was in the air, the Aldens settled in. It felt just like a normal flight, except the booming of the engines was louder.

"I was thinking about something," Violet said while they listened to the plane's engines. "In the riddle, there was a part about how Antarctica was a rumor for hundreds of years. Do you know anything about that, Aunt Jane?"

Aunt Jane nodded. "Yes, a little. Early explorers were unable to travel all the way south because their ships couldn't stand up to the cold."

"Like the Reddimus jet," Benny said.

"Right, just like the jet. So, for a long time, people from all different parts of the world saw only glimpses. Many people guessed that there was land at the South Pole, but no one could prove it."

"Wow, just think of it!" Violet said. "A mysterious continent. It's funny to think that whole thing was just a rumor for so long."

Their conversation had caught the ear of the flight attendant sitting nearby. It was the same attendant who had checked them in at the airport. Now that they were relaxing on the plane, Benny could read his name tag. It said *Brian*.

"Isn't it interesting?" Brian asked. "And there is still a lot we don't know about Antarctica and other parts of the world. That's why so many of the people who go to Antarctica are researchers."

"How long is the flight?" Benny asked.

"In a C-17 like this one, only about six hours..." Brian replied. He tilted his head, trailing off. "I just remembered. The woman who dropped off your coats and gear told me to tell you something...What was it?...Oh yes! She told me to remind you to watch where you sit. Do you know what it means?"

"Watch where we sit?" Henry repeated. "We've already sat down."

"Watch could also mean that we should look,"

Violet said. "Benny, can you see anything under our chairs?"

Benny leaned forward and looked under his seat. There was nothing there, so he peered under Aunt Jane's, Violet's, Jessie's, and Henry's too. He could see something taped to the underside of Henry's chair.

"Henry, there's something under your chair," he said. "It looks like an envelope!"

Henry reached down. Benny was right: there was an envelope taped below his seat. It had a familiar logo with an *R* and an owl drawn on the front of it. Inside was a series of photographs.

"What is it?" Aunt Jane asked. Brian leaned forward to look too.

"Some photos of people with flags," Henry said, puzzled. He handed the photos to Jessie, who looked and handed them to Benny and Violet. "I don't know exactly what they mean yet, but I do get the feeling they are our next clue."

Shackleton's Semaphore

The Aldens took turns looking at the photos. Each one was of a man in parka standing on what looked like an airplane runway, except it was covered in snow. The man was holding two flags, one in each hand. The only thing different about the photographs was that in each one, the man was holding the flags in different positions.

Each photo also had a number written on the bottom corner in permanent marker. The numbers went from one to fourteen. Benny put all the photos in order.

"It must be some kind of message," he said. "But what?"

"The flags must be some kind of signal," Jessie

suggested. "Do you remember? When we were at the airport, I saw people using light batons to direct the planes. This man holding the flags looks like that."

"Maybe it's a version of air traffic control," Henry said. "Say, Brian. Do you know anything about this?"

Benny, who was sitting closest to Brian, showed him one of the photographs.

"Do you know what this might mean?" he asked.

Brian flipped through the photographs and nodded. "I do. I mean, I think I know what these are, but I don't know what they say. You see, I think these are letters in semaphore."

"Letters?" Violet asked.

"Semaphore?" Jessie added. "What's semaphore? Is it a language?"

"Sort of!" said Brian. "Semaphore is a way of spelling out letters using the positions of flags. It's a way of sending a message over a long distance without using a telephone or radio. It's used by the navy, for example, to send short messages from ship to ship. You can see from the photographs that these flags are very bright. It would be easy to see them from far away."

"So the different flag positions represent different letters?" Henry asked. "Great! Then all we need to do is find someone who knows how to decode semaphore and ask them to help us write down which letter each photograph represents!"

"Do you think anyone on the plane might know how to decode it?" Jessie asked.

Brian tapped his chin with a finger. "Hmm... You know, there just might be. There are a few passengers here who work with the US Air Force and the US Navy. I'll bet at least one of them would be able to help you. Wait here and I will go and ask."

Brian unbuckled his safety belt and walked through the plane, holding on to the hand straps and chairs to keep his balance. He asked if any of the passengers knew anything about semaphore. At first, it seemed like no one would be able to help them.

"I wonder if there's Wi-Fi at McMurdo Station," Jessie said. "We could probably look up the letters of the semaphore code online. But for right now, I hope there is someone on the plane who might be able to help us."

Brian got to the last row of passengers. Just when it seemed like they were out of luck, Brian spoke to an older man who looked up and nodded. Brian explained and the man waved at the Aldens. A minute later, he came over to take an empty seat next to them.

"I heard you could use some help decoding semaphore," he said. "My name is Stephen Liau. I was a doctor in the navy, where we learned semaphore. It's been a while, but I could probably help you."

"That would be great!" Benny said. He handed over the photographs. Jessie found her notebook and pencil and offered those too. While Dr. Liau looked at the photographs and wrote in Jessie's notebook, Aunt Jane asked, "What brings you to Antarctica?"

"I'm retired, but some of my nephews work for an Antarctic program. When I was in the navy, I traveled all over the world. I have been to all the continents except Antarctica, so I decided to make the trip!"

"Antarctica is our sixth continent," Violet said. "We've been traveling a lot lately."

Dr. Liau was almost done going through the photographs.

"Good for you," he said. "Traveling is wonderful for the mind and spirit. You learn so many things when you see how big the world really is...and, in some ways, how small! Here you go. I couldn't remember one of the positions, but I think you might still be able to figure out what it says."

Dr. Liau handed the photos back to Benny and the notebook back to Jessie.

"Thank you!" said Benny.

"No, thank you," said Dr. Liau. "It was fun to exercise my memory. It's not every day you get to read a message in semaphore!"

Dr. Liau waved good-bye and went back to his seat. The Aldens looked at the letters from the semaphore message. One letter, the letter Dr. Liau couldn't remember, was missing:

SHACKLETONS H_T

"Shackletons?" Henry said. "What are Shackletons?"

"It's a name!" Jessie exclaimed. "Ernest Shackleton. I read about him when I was reading about explorers. He spent many years exploring Antarctica and trying to reach the South Pole."

"So what is the second word?" Benny asked. "Maybe...hat?"

Henry nodded. "It could be *Shackleton's hat*. I'm sure he wore hats on his adventures, because it was so cold."

"*Shackleton's hit* doesn't make any sense," Violet said. "And it couldn't be *Shackleton's hot* because it's not hot in Antarctica at all."

"*Shackleton's hat* could be it," Jessie agreed. "But I don't understand yet how it helps us return the biscuit tin from the Reddimus box. Maybe when we get to McMurdo Station, the clue will make more sense."

"Wait a second," Aunt Jane said. "If it was *Shackleton's hat*, we would know. There's an *A* in *Shackleton*. So, if it were *hat*, the same flag position would have been used there too."

"So it's not *hat*?" Benny asked. He was a little confused, so Henry took out the photographs of the flags again. They lined the photographs up in order, and Henry pointed to the third photograph, which stood for the A in *Shackleton*.

"Oh, I see what Aunt Jane is saying," Henry said. "Look here. The flag position in this photo means A. But it's different from the one that Dr. Liau can't remember. That means that the letter in between H and T is not A."

"Oh!" Benny said. Now he understood. He looked at the photos some more. "Then it's not *het* or *hot* either. The E and O are both in *Shackleton* too. But those flags don't match the one between the H and T either."

"And *hit* still doesn't make any sense," Violet said.

"What about *hut*?" Jessie asked. "Shackleton's Hut! Maybe Ernest Shackleton had a hut where he lived when he wasn't exploring."

Benny nodded. That made sense. "Maybe that's where he kept all his biscuits!" he said.

They spent the rest of the plane ride practicing the semaphore from the photographs. They didn't have flags so they used pieces of paper from Jessie's notebook. There weren't many letters to work with, but she was still able to spell some words: *cat*, *note*, and *sack*. Benny had a fun time matching the flag positions to the letters using the photos, and Jessie helped him sound out the words.

When it was Henry's turn to spell a word, he wrote out SOS.

"What's S-O-S?" Benny asked. He tried to sound it out. "Soss?"

"SOS doesn't actually stand for anything," Henry explained. "It's a signal that means there is an emergency. If you were stranded on a deserted island, you might try to write SOS in the sand in case a plane flew by. Then they would know you needed help."

"SOS is a good thing to be able to spell in semaphore," Violet said. "You could use it to signal for help on a ship or to a plane, even if you didn't have a cell phone or a radio."

"I want to practice SOS using the flags," Benny said. "But I hope we never have to use it from a deserted island!"

"Don't worry, Benny. I don't think we will," Aunt

Jane assured him. "This plane is very safe. The Reddimus Society has taken very good care of us on our journey."

"Now if only we could find out which pilot is spying on us," Henry said. It was a relief to talk about this now, when they didn't have to worry about being overheard. "After we return the biscuit tin, we should figure out which of the pilots is working for the Argents."

"I was just thinking about that," said Jessie, "when we were trying to figure out the mystery letter in the semaphore riddle. At first, when we thought it might say *hat*, I was thinking about all the ways we might try to find Ernest Shackleton's hat. But when we realized it said *hut*, I had to change my plans to imagine a hut instead. Depending on how we thought about the message, we could have gone on two very different adventures. I wonder if we can use that idea to figure out which of the pilots is working for the Argents."

"The Argents led us on a fake adventure already," Violet said. "When they gave us the fake message about Thailand and tried to trick us into giving the artifact to the wrong person."

"But if we give both pilots a message and send them both on a fake adventure, then we won't have anyone to fly the jet," Benny said. "Then we would have to signal SOS for the Silvertons to send us new pilots!"

Jessie sighed. It was a difficult problem to solve. There had to be a way to single out the Argent spy. If they thought about it, they would be able to figure it out.

"People will do different things depending on what information they get," she said. "Just like with our message about Shackleton's Hut when we thought it might say Shackleton's hat."

"What if we gave them two different messages and watch what they do?" Violet suggested. "But I don't know what kind of message would show us which one of them is a spy for the Argents. It's not like we can say, 'If you are the spy, then tell us right away.'"

Benny giggled at that idea. "That would be too easy," he said. "Anyway, if they knew the message came from us, then they would know we were trying to figure them out. We're going to have to be clever to outsmart them!"

"Yes, we will," Henry said. "Let's all keep thinking about it. But don't forget we need to return the biscuit tin first. After we do that, we can work more on figuring out which pilot is working for the Argents."

CHAPTER 9

Returning the Sixth Artifact

Before long, the captain's voice came over the intercom and announced that the plane was nearing McMurdo Station. The children bundled up in their parkas and put on the rest of their warm clothes. Benny put on his goggles and grinned from ear to ear.

"Boy, am I glad we're covered from head to toe!" Jessie said as they left the plane. The wind was as cold as the inside of a freezer as it blew icy needles at them across the snowy McMurdo Station runway. In the distance they could see boxy, square buildings in front of what looked like a mountain of snow. Everywhere they looked was snow and ice. Their breath clouded in the air.

Returning the Sixth Artifact

The Aldens followed the researchers and boarded a red bus that took them from the runway to the buildings that they had seen. McMurdo Station was not just one station building but a small town, with dirt roads covered in snow. Everyone they passed was wearing a parka and hat and heavy-duty boots.

"Jasper told me he would pick us up," Aunt Jane said.

"Do you want to call him and let him know we're here?" Jessie asked, offering her phone.

"I would, but there's no signal here! Jasper and I both remember what it's like to make plans before cell phones were around. It's good to do things the old-fashioned way sometimes!"

Aunt Jane was right. They did not have to wait too long. A truck drove up and out came a man in a purple parka. Benny noticed him right away. "There!" Benny shouted and pointed.

The man smiled and tromped over in his snow boots. He gave Aunt Jane a hug.

"Jane, it's so good to see you! You look well! And you must be Henry, Jessie, Violet, and Benny!" Jasper shook their hands, which was a funny feeling wearing the parkas and thick mittens. "Welcome to McMurdo Station. I'm Jasper Chandra. I am a historian here at McMurdo...among other things. We all do many jobs here to keep everything up and running. Anyway, let's get you somewhere warm."

Jasper drove the truck to a building with a row of flags from many different countries posted out front. When the Aldens got inside, it was much warmer. It was nice enough that they could take off their hats and gloves and unzip their parkas.

"Most of the people doing research here are working on projects in earth and space sciences," Jasper said. "Because I am a historian, I do much of my research here at the headquarters."

"Thanks for picking us up," Aunt Jane said. "I'm sorry it had to be under mysterious circumstances, but the children are working on an important project and their plans can't be accidentally shared with the wrong people."

Jasper blinked, looking confused. "Yes, of course, I understand...You do *know*, don't you?"

It was the Aldens' turn to be confused. Jessie tilted her head.

"Know what?" she asked.

Jasper gestured to his purple parka. Then he took an envelope out of his pocket and showed them the back. Stamped on the corner was the Reddimus logo. "I'm afraid there must have been a misunderstanding. I'm a friend of owls...you know, your contact here in Antarctica?"

"What?" cried Benny. "Aunt Jane! You didn't tell us your friend worked with the Reddimus Society!"

Aunt Jane was just as surprised. "I couldn't tell you what I didn't know! Jasper, how long have you known that I was coming, and that my grandnieces and grandnephews were helping the Reddimus Society?"

Jasper laughed. It seemed like he enjoyed surprising them.

"Oh, not long. Yesterday I got this message saying I would see an old friend soon, and that she would be helping four little owls return something that had been stolen. When I heard you were coming this way, I knew it had to be you. Come on, let's go to my office and sit down."

Jasper took them to his office, which was

modest and organized. He had many books and a few old-looking items sitting out on the shelves. Everything was tidy and taken care of. It was nice to see that the Reddimus Society really did have members all over the world—even all the way in Antarctica.

"Speaking of the item that was stolen," Jasper went on, "do you know anything about it yet, or will we be going on our own expedition? I wouldn't want Jane to have all the mystery-solving fun."

"We know a few things," said Henry. He took out the camera case and revealed the box with the biscuit tin. He showed Jasper and told him about the semaphore clue and the message it had contained: Shackleton's Hut. "Do you know what it means, or what the connection might be?"

Jasper had a funny smile on his face. "Yes," he said. "In fact, I do. It was very clever of our clue-giver to use semaphore to tell you about Shackleton's Hut. You see, Sir Ernest Shackleton was an expert at using semaphore. He often taught his crew members to signal using flags to pass the time. So I'm happy you solved the puzzle and that it also brings you to visit Shackleton's Hut."

"You know what the hut refers to?" Jessie asked.

"Yes. Shackleton had a base on Ross Island, for his Nimrod Expedition. He built a lot of bases, because he went on many expeditions during his career, but this one for whatever reason has gone down in history as Shackleton's Hut. It is tremendously interesting for a historian like me, and I'm sure the four of you would be glad to see it as well."

"What about the biscuit tin?" Benny asked. "We are used to returning the artifacts to museums, but I didn't see any museums on our drive here."

"No, there aren't any museums like the ones you might visit in other parts of the world," Jasper said. "However, Shackleton's Hut, as well as other sites here in Antarctica, are protected by different organizations as historical sites. They are preserved the way we found them. So, in a way, visiting them is like visiting a museum, because everything is just the way it was."

Jasper pulled out a memo from his desk and showed it to the Aldens.

The Shackleton Sabotage

"I received this a few months ago. Someone was doing an inventory of Shackleton's Hut and found that several items were missing. It's strange for things to go missing out here because almost no one would fly all the way here just to steal a few items. However, some people must have known that some of the items are valuable. And the biscuits that were stolen—which I imagine you have in that tin right there—are very valuable indeed. Other biscuits like them have been sold for thousands of dollars."

Benny gasped. "A thousand-dollar cracker! Boy, I'm glad I didn't eat it!"

"It sounds like we're here to return the biscuit tin to Shackleton's Hut then," Violet said. She handed the tin to Jasper. "I'm sure you'll take good care of it!"

Jasper nodded, but he didn't take the tin.

"You know, it would be a shame for you to fly all the way here just to leave without seeing anything. Why don't you come with me to Shackleton's Hut and return the tin in person? I think you would all enjoy seeing the hut, especially if you're interested in history like I am."

"That sounds wonderful!" Jessie exclaimed. "Aunt Jane, is it all right?"

"Absolutely!" Aunt Jane said. "After reading all of Jasper's emails about this place, there's no way I would leave without seeing at least some of it with my own eyes."

"Excellent. Then I'll make arrangements for the helicopter," Jasper said. "The forecast for tomorrow looks good, so we should be able to fly out first thing in the morning."

"Are there hotels in Antarctica?" Benny asked. It had been a long day, and he was getting tired.

"Not really. But we have dormitories, and Tricia mentioned you would need a place to stay."

Jasper took them to a brown building a short drive away from the research headquarters. The dormitory building was raised up on concrete blocks. It was a very simple building, but the inside was warm. Jasper had the keys for two dorm rooms that were across the hall from each other, and he gave them to the children and Aunt Jane.

"A cafeteria, laundry, and showers are in the building, so make yourselves at home," he said.

"And for Jane, a coffeemaker! Now, I need to wrap up a few things so I can take the time off tomorrow to visit Shackleton's Hut with you. I'll see you in the morning."

Jasper said good-bye, and the children unlocked the doors to the two dorms. The rooms were small, each with one set of bunk beds and a couch. Henry checked his watch while Violet and Benny explored the rooms. Jessie and Aunt Jane took off their coats.

"I just noticed...it's night, but the sun is still shining," Henry said.

Jessie pulled the curtains back from the small window. "You're right. I didn't realize it because I'm still a little jet-lagged from all our flying."

"How are we going to go to bed if the sun is up?" Benny asked, yawning. It didn't actually look like he was going to have any problems falling asleep. Jessie smiled and pulled the curtains shut. They were so heavy that all the light from outside was blocked.

"They're used to it here, remember? These light-blocking curtains will make it just as dark as nighttime in Connecticut."

Returning the Sixth Artifact

Jessie was right. With the curtains shut, it was easy to fall asleep—especially after all they'd done that day.

The next morning, the weather was fair, with the sun shining just as it had the previous evening. They got ready for their day, and just as Aunt Jane was finishing her morning coffee, they heard a friendly honk. Violet looked out the window and saw Jasper's truck waiting outside. They bundled up and went out into the chilly morning to meet him.

"Good morning!" Jasper said as they climbed in the warmed-up truck. "The pilot said the weather is all clear, so we're good to go."

Neither the children nor Aunt Jane had ever ridden in a helicopter before. They forgot all about the cold when they saw it on the helipad. They wore earmuffs over their hats so the thrumming sound of the helicopter's engine didn't hurt their ears. Jasper waved to the pilot once they were on board, and the helicopter lifted off the ground and headed for Shackleton's Hut.

Riding in a helicopter was much different from

riding in an airplane. The cabin was so small that it seemed much more like they were flying than it did when they looked out the window of an airplane. Antarctica was covered in white snow as far as the eye could see. When the helicopter began to descend, Benny pointed out the window.

"Look at all the penguins!" he said.

There were penguin colonies up and down the coast. It was fun to see the penguins in their natural habitat after seeing them at the aquarium.

"That must be the hut," Jessie said. On a rocky, snow-covered area near where the penguins were roosting was an old-fashioned, rectangular wood house.

"It looks just like a cabin in Connecticut," Aunt Jane said.

The helicopter landed and the children followed Jasper across the packed ice that crunched under their feet. Penguins darted around them squawking. "They sound like they're warning their friends we're coming!" Benny said and laughed.

Inside the hut reminded Jessie even more of a cabin in the woods, though they were far away

from the woods in Connecticut where they had camped in their boxcar. Like the boxcar, the hut was a single room. The walls were made of wood panels and lined with shelves. All of the shelves had jars and cans of food. On one end of the room was an old, iron stove. It was dim inside because there were no lights, and it smelled like cedar, old sleeping bags, and dust.

"Because of how cold it is, many of the things here have been preserved remarkably well," said Jasper while the children and Aunt Jane looked around. "It is amazing what Shackleton accomplished, especially in his day and age."

"It's like we've stepped back in time," Violet said. "Look, there's even some old socks still hanging here to dry!"

After they were done exploring the hut, Henry took out the biscuit tin.

"Let's find where this goes and put it back," he said.

They searched along the shelves until Benny found a tin that matched the one Henry was holding.

"They had a whole stack of biscuits," Benny said. "They were probably keeping them to sell when they got back from their exploring."

"They probably weren't worth thousands of dollars back then," joked Henry. He carefully placed the biscuit tin from the Reddimus box on the top of the stack. They all gazed at the stack of tins in the old pantry shelf and smiled.

"Good work," Jasper said. "I'm very proud of you for coming so far to return this item. Thank you on behalf of all members of the Reddimus Society."

It seemed almost silly that Jasper would thank them for returning a tin of biscuits, but looking around, the Aldens knew that it meant a lot. History was not always grand and dramatic. The tin of biscuits in the remote hut were very different from the Egyptian pyramids and the Great Wall of China. Still they were an important part of history, and now the little part that had gone missing had been returned, and the historical monument was whole again.

They waved good-bye to the penguins, and the helicopter took them back to McMurdo Station, where they warmed up and rested before their flight back to Christchurch. Jasper treated them to hot cocoa, and Aunt Jane had a nice cup of hot coffee. While they waited, they told Jasper about their travels so far. He whistled with admiration.

"By the time you are done, you will have seen more of the world than me!" he said. "Mrs. Silverton will be very proud. Perhaps they will ask you to join the Reddimus Society."

"That would be a great honor," Henry said. "But first we would have to finish school."

"I don't want spring break to end," Benny said.

Jessie laughed. "Oh, Benny. If our spring break has been so wonderful, just imagine what our summer vacation will be like!"

Jasper drove them back to the airfield when it was time for their flight. He waved good-bye and made sure they boarded safely.

"Safe journey!" he called. "And good luck with the last artifact!"

CHAPTER 10

The Man in the Red Hat

The flight back to Christchurch was rough. The plane shuddered and rocked, and the flight attendants made an announcement over the speaker system.

"Because the weather is changing, please wear your safety belts at all times."

Benny squeezed Aunt Jane's hand when the turbulence shook the whole plane.

"We'll be fine, Benny. These planes are sturdy and can handle any kind of weather."

"If you say so," Benny mumbled. He wasn't feeling so great.

"Benny, I've got something good to distract you," Henry said. "I think I have a plan to test

Emilio and Mr. Ganert. Do you want to hear the plan?"

"Yes!" said Benny. He wanted to talk about anything but the bumpy plane ride. "Tell me the plan!"

"Jessie was talking about how different people do different things based on how they understand messages. I think we can use messages to find out which pilot is sending information to the Argents."

"We use messages to trick the spy into saying so?" Benny said and squeezed Jessie's hand again.

"But the spy won't do a spy thing while we're watching," Violet said. "That would give them away."

"Right," Henry said. "But what's the one thing the spy has been trying to do?"

"Steal the artifacts!" Benny said.

"And how has the spy been doing that?" Henry asked.

"By reading our messages and figuring out the answers to all the riddles," Jessie said, catching on. "If we wrote fake messages and pretended the messages were from the Reddimus Society, both the pilots would think they were real. Then, the real spy would try to take advantage of that. But that still doesn't help us figure out which one is the spy."

"That's why we will write *two* fake messages," Henry said. "Like the Shackleton message. The messages will be mostly the same, but slightly different. We will make it seem like the next step is an easy chance to trick us into giving up the last artifact. I'll show you."

Henry took out two notes he had been working on. He had written them in very fine penmanship. The first note said: *Go to the airport hotel restaurant. You will be approached by a man in RED hat. Give him the seventh box. He will deliver it for you.*

The second note said: *Go to the airport hotel restaurant. You will be approached by a man in GREEN hat. Give him the seventh box. He will deliver it for you.*

"They're the same except for the color of the hat," Violet noticed.

"Precisely. Now, if you were an Argent spy and you saw that we were given this first set of instructions, what would you try to do?" Henry asked with a clever smile.

"I would hire a thief to wear a red hat and go to the hotel restaurant," Jessie said. "But if I were the Argent spy and I received the second note, I would hire a thief to wear a green hat."

Henry nodded. "We will give Mr. Ganert the first message and Emilio the second."

"So, we just remember which pilot gets which message," Violet finished. "And then when we go to the restaurant, if we are approached by someone in a red or a green hat, we will know which pilot is trying to steal the artifact from us!"

"Because really there is no man in a hat coming to deliver the box for us!" Benny exclaimed. It was a complicated plan, and he was happy with how clever it was. "If it's a man in a green hat, we'll know Emilio is trying to steal the artifact. But if it's a man in a red hat, we'll know the spy is Mr. Ganert."

"You got it, Benny," Henry said. "It's the little changes in the message that make all the difference. Just like *Shackleton's Hut* and *Shackleton's Hat*."

Aunt Jane had been listening in while they

worked out their plan. She raised her eyebrows and nodded proudly. "Clever boy, Henry!" she said.

Henry put the finishing touches on his notes during the rest of the flight. He reused two old Reddimus envelopes and sealed them so they looked very official. Then on both of the envelopes, he wrote, "Do not open" and "Deliver to the Aldens immediately." He addressed the envelope that contained the message about the man in the red hat to Mr. Ganert, and he addressed the envelope that contained the message about the man in the green hat to Emilio.

"We will deliver them secretly, so the pilots don't suspect the message came from us," Henry explained. "If we hand the envelopes to them directly, the spy might be suspicious that we are on to him."

When the plane finally landed in Christchurch, Aunt Jane found several missed messages on her cell phone. They were all from Grandfather. The Aldens waited while she listened. When she was done listening to the voice messages, she laughed to herself.

"Your grandfather sounds lonely without the four of you to keep him company," she explained.

"When's the last time you visited with him?" Jessie asked. She couldn't help but notice Aunt Jane was looking a bit tired from all the traveling. Although she had been eager to travel with her nieces and nephews, all the flights and hiking were a lot, especially for someone Aunt Jane's age. Even Jessie felt a bit sore from it sometimes.

"I suppose it's been a while," Aunt Jane said.

"Then why don't you fly to Greenfield and visit?" Violet suggested, noticing what Jessie was noticing.

"Oh, no! I wouldn't leave you on your own. Especially with those pesky pilots."

Henry smiled. He had noticed that Aunt Jane looked a little tired too. "Don't worry, Aunt Jane. We've got a plan. We really enjoyed having you with us and spending time with you. But we also want to make sure you have a chance to rest!"

"And we don't want Grandfather to be very lonely or bored," Benny added. "Will you go home and let him know we miss him?"

Aunt Jane seemed reluctant to leave them, but she also knew they could take care of themselves. They were resourceful and had already done plenty of traveling on their own. With a bittersweet sigh, she nodded.

"I would be happy to explore with the four of you until the cows came home," she said. "But I think you're right. Your grandfather might get into trouble without someone to keep him company, so I will give you all four big hugs and see you when you come home. After you've returned that last artifact, of course!"

"Of course!" they said together.

Aunt Jane gave them those four big hugs and they said good-bye. Henry called Emilio to find out where the pilots were staying. Emilio was at the airport hotel, while Mr. Ganert had stayed in the Reddimus jet's on-board suite.

"This is great news," Henry said. "This way it will be easy for us to deliver the two different messages without the pilots knowing. Violet and I will bring one letter to Mr. Ganert. Jessie, you and Benny bring the other letter to Emilio at the airport hotel.

Then Violet and I will meet you at the hotel to see how our plan works out."

Jessie nodded and took the letter that was for Emilio. The four Aldens split into two groups and went to deliver their messages. Emilio had checked out two rooms, one for himself and one for the Aldens. Jessie and Benny went to his room, slipped the envelope under his door, and hurried away before he could come out and see them. Afterward, they checked in to their own hotel room.

Henry and Violet met them in the hotel room later.

"Did you do it?" asked Benny. "Did you deliver the letter to Mr. Ganert?"

"Did he know it was you?" asked Jessie.

"No, he did not," Violet said proudly. "We snuck onto the plane and left it taped to the door of the sleeping suite."

"We left without him even waking up," Henry said. "How about you two?"

"We slipped Emilio's letter under his door. It's a little ways down the hall," Jessie said. Henry nodded and looked pleased.

"Great. Now we just have to wait."

After changing out of their heavy-duty Antarctic gear, they relaxed in the hotel room and waited for one of the pilots to give them a call. Benny was nervous. It was hard to wait to find out which of the pilots was working against them, but Jessie reminded Benny that once they found out, it would be easier to decide what to do so they could safely deliver the last artifact.

The first call came from Mr. Ganert.

"Are you back in New Zealand?" he asked without saying hello.

"We're back from Antarctica," Henry replied. "We've returned the sixth Reddimus artifact, and we've already checked in to the hotel."

"I received a message for you. Meet me in the hotel restaurant."

He hung up without saying good-bye. A moment later, the phone rang again. This time it was Emilio.

"How was your trip?" asked Emilio. Henry told Emilio the same thing he had told Mr. Ganert a moment ago.

"Oh, wonderful!" said Emilio. "Listen, I received

a message for you while I was taking a nap. Are you all getting hungry for supper? I can meet you in the hotel restaurant if you want to get something to eat."

After Henry hung up, the Aldens exchanged determined glances at one another. It was time to find out if their plan would work.

"Ready?" Jessie asked.

"Ready!" said Benny and Violet together.

They went down to the hotel restaurant. Benny was glad about this because he was so hungry he felt like he could eat an iceberg. The pilots didn't come to the restaurant right away, so the children ordered and waited for their meals.

"I hope Mr. Ganert is the Argent spy," Benny said while they waited. "I like Emilio and his goofy jokes."

After a little while, both Emilio and Mr. Ganert came to the restaurant and found the Aldens at their table.

"Hello! Would you look at this? We both received messages for you," Emilio said.

Mr. Ganert, who looked neither happy nor sad

about the messages, added, "You should read these messages right away. They are probably clues to returning the last artifact."

Henry took the envelopes from Mr. Ganert and Emilio. He pretended as if he had never seen them before. He handed one of the envelopes to Jessie, and they read the messages quietly.

"Yes, they are clues," Henry said. "Thank you for bringing them to us! Soon we will know what to do."

Mr. Ganert looked around anxiously. He seemed to be waiting for something to happen. Emilio only waved for Mr. Ganert to leave with him.

"Let's head back to the jet and let the Aldens work on the clues in peace," he said. "They are clever kids, cleverer than us. I'm sure we'll soon hear the next destination for the final artifact."

Mr. Ganert frowned but nodded. "Very well. But make sure to do what the Reddimus Society suggests. We don't want the artifacts falling into the wrong hands."

After Emilio and Mr. Ganert left, Violet let out a little sigh.

"I'm so nervous," she said. "But I'm excited too! I'm ready to know which of them it is at last."

"In the meantime, let's try to enjoy our dinner," Jessie said.

They did. The hotel had delicious food, and for a little while, Violet forgot that they were waiting for a man in a red or green hat to find them. No matter what color hat the man wore, he would be a thief, sent by either Mr. Ganert or Emilio.

It happened while they were eating dessert. Benny was scooping up a spoonful of ice cream when he saw a man in a baseball cap enter the restaurant. The man looked around, and when he saw the children at the table, he walked toward them.

"Here he comes!" Benny whispered. "He's wearing a red hat!"

"So it's Mr. Ganert!" gasped Violet. "Henry, what will we do when he gets here?"

"I will take care of it," Henry said.

The man came up to the table and adjusted his cap, as if to make sure the children saw that he was wearing it even though it was bright red and hard to miss.

"Hello," the man said. "I am a friend of the owls…"

"A friend of the owls?" Henry said. "What do you mean by that?"

The man looked flustered.

"Er, I…isn't that the secret code?"

"Secret code for what?" Jessie asked, winking at Henry and playing along.

"Aren't you the Alden children?" the man asked. "Don't you have a box for me?"

"No, we don't," said Violet. "I'm afraid you've been tricked."

"That's right. We haven't got any box for you," Benny added loudly. His voice got the attention of some of the other guests at the restaurant.

The man in the red hat didn't know what to do. His cheeks turned as red as his hat when he realized everyone in the restaurant was looking at him.

"Is there a problem?" asked the restaurant manager, coming over.

"Oh," mumbled the man. "No, it's all right. My mistake…"

Looking over his shoulder, he slunk out of the

restaurant. The Aldens gave each other high fives. They had done it! They had figured out that Mr. Ganert was the Argent spy. The thief wearing the red hat was proof.

After dinner, the Aldens went to their hotel room. They had spent a lot of time strapped into airplane seats, and stretching out in the comfortable hotel was a welcome change. As they relaxed, they tried to make a plan for how to deal with Mr. Ganert.

"Will Mr. Ganert know that we found him out when the man in the red hat comes back empty-handed?" Violet asked.

"If he's suspicious, we will tell him we got another clue at the last minute that told us not to give the box to anyone," Henry said. "Anyway, he won't be able to say very much about it without giving away his secret. If we pretend everything is normal, he will have little choice but to do the same."

"We should tell Trudy right away," Jessie said. "Hopefully she can use it to prove that Tricia isn't the one giving information to the Argents."

But before they could call Trudy, someone knocked on the door. "Room service!" a voice called from outside. Benny went to see what it was. In the hallway was a cart with a little glass jar on the top. Benny brought it in and showed it to the others.

"What is it?" Violet asked. "It looks like caramel."

The contents of the jar were light brown and very thick. The label on the jar read *Dulce de Leche*. There was also a note tied to the neck of the jar with a string. The note simply said, "Fair Winds."

Violet opened the jar and gave the sticky contents a sniff. "Mmm!" she said. "It smells sweet!"

"Dulce de leche," Jessie said, reading the label again. "Oh yes! It's Spanish. We tried some in my Spanish class. It means 'sweet of milk.' It's a traditional Spanish dessert ingredient."

"It must be a clue to our last destination—some place where Spanish is spoken. The note that says 'Fair Winds' must be part of the clue too," Henry added. He was surprised they had gotten their next clue so soon, but that just meant they would get to travel again first thing in the morning. It would be the start of their journey to return the final Reddimus artifact. Jessie nodded.

"Let's figure out where we're headed to right away!" she said.

"Wherever we're going next," Benny said, "I'm sure they have great desserts!"

GERTRUDE CHANDLER WARNER discovered when she was teaching that many readers who like an exciting story could find no books that were both easy and fun to read. She decided to try to meet this need, and her first book, *The Boxcar Children*, quickly proved she had succeeded.

Miss Warner drew on her own experiences to write the mystery. As a child she spent hours watching trains go by on the tracks opposite her family home. She often dreamed about what it would be like to set up housekeeping in a caboose or freight car—the situation the Alden children find themselves in.

While the mystery element is central to each of Miss Warner's books, she never thought of them as strictly juvenile mysteries. She liked to stress the Aldens' independence and resourcefulness and their solid New England devotion to using up and making do. The Aldens go about most of their adventures with as little adult supervision as possible—something else that delights young readers.

Miss Warner lived in Putnam, Connecticut, until her death in 1979. During her lifetime, she received hundreds of letters from girls and boys telling her how much they liked her books.